DAUGHTER OF THE WILDS

CAITLIN HOONEFIELD

First Printing, 2019

ISBN -13:978-0-578-52563-1

Amazon Kindle Direct Publishing

To my husband, and family, especially my cousins.
Without our adventures, my stories wouldn't be the same.

List of Characters

Avana — Main character, human, daughter of Caleb, and descendant of the kings of old

Aramis — Human, Avana's grandfather, and head Ranger

Killian — Dwarf, nephew to King Halfor

Caleb — Human, Avana's father, kidnapped by goblins, and former Ranger

Kalmar — Dwarf, Killian's father, and brother of Halfor

Zyphereth — Dwarf, Killian's mother

Commander Ruskin — Human, High Commander of the army of the city of Amaroth

Captain Marco — Captain in the Guard of Amaroth

Captain Grayson — Avana's uncle, half dwarf, half human

Svengale — Human, one of Avana's core group of soldiers, from the North; a wise and fierce fighter

Halfor — King of the dwarves

Halever — Dwarf prince and son of Halfor; gets kidnapped by goblins

Garzvahl — Chief of all the goblins

Finris — Chief of all the Wolves of the North, adopted father of Avana

Fallon — Son of Finris, Avana's adopted wolf brother

Valanter — Elven king, lives in the Greenwood Forest

Zellnar — Dragon of Lonrach Lake

Nedanael — Elf, master craftsman of weapons

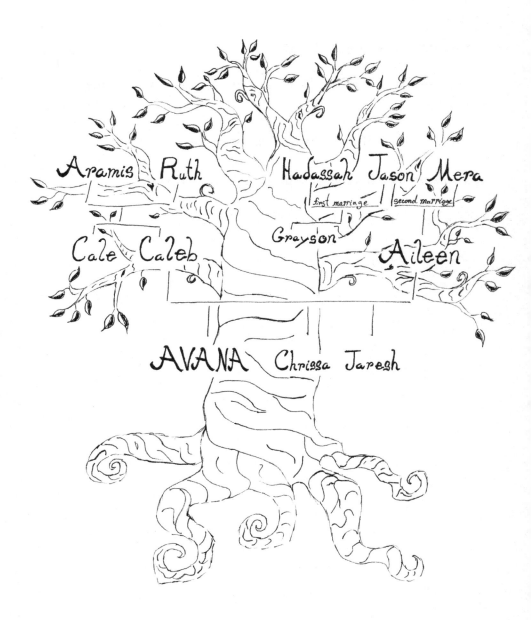

TABLE OF CONTENTS

PROLOGUE
FIVE HUNDRED YEARS EARLIER

THE FIRE RAGED ACROSS THE CITY, jumping from roof to roof. It was unstoppable. Goblins and pirates from the North chased the terrified citizens through the streets. The army of Amaroth was all but decimated after the deadly attacks. A few brave soldiers stood outside the gates of the castle and battled desperately in a final attempt to defend the royal family. Behind them, half the palace was already engulfed. Horses screamed in high pitched whinnies as the doors to the royal stables were thrown open to allow the frightened animals loose followed by grooms and stable hands. In their flight, the horses ran frantically through the side roads, trampling both humans and goblins.

Inside the castle, the few servants who remained were in a frenzy to evacuate the royal family. The King and Queen, with their four small children, retreated to the far end of the castle, the only unburnt section, through a passage that emptied to the vegetable gardens. The open air was filled with smoke, and flames licked at the ceiling behind them, mocking them.

Then they all heard the familiar flap of wings. A dragon—a loyal friend, thank the Lord—wheeled through the sky and landed on the other side of the garden wall. Matthew, the footman, cried out in dismay when he saw vicious goblins surround Zellnar the Dragon inside the castle walls. Drawing his sword, he rushed headlong into the fray.

The King called out to Zellnar, "Matthew and I can hold off the goblins. Please save my wife and children."

Blasting the goblins with a fiery stream, Zellnar cleared a space around him for the Queen and children to approach, setting down his starboard wing for the family to climb aboard his back. "I will come back for you, Justinian," Zellnar spoke fiercely to the King.

"Don't worry about me," Justinian replied as he fought alongside Matthew. "Just get my family out of here!"

With a powerful thrust of his wings, Zellnar sent another deadly blast over the goblins, incinerating dozens. This diversion gave the King and Matthew a real chance at escape.

CHAPTER 1

THE DWARVES HAD BEEN TRAVELING ALL DAY through the foothills of the Wilds, and now the sun cast long shadows on the uneven ground. The road from the Cascade Mountains to the Western Sea across the land of Arda was long and treacherous, but the dwarves were returning home and so hurried their steps, pushing onward into the night. Suddenly, the scout ahead waved the company to a halt, motioning their leader to join him. Together, they left the road and crept slowly into the surrounding rocks and brush as darkness settled over them.

The sounds of clashing swords and armor rang out louder and louder as they drew closer to the lip of a deep dell. Stealthily peeking over it, they were surprised by the sight below—a human girl, around eighteen years of age, fought ferociously, surrounded by a dozen goblins that had backed her against the wall of the dell. A small campfire to the left was the girl's only other source of protection besides the great sword she so skillfully wielded. The fire cast an eerie glow on the scene as the goblins laughed and jeered at her predicament. Rushing at her in twos and threes, they harassed her relentlessly.

In an unspoken agreement, the dwarf scouts quietly hastened back to the rest of their party to alert them to the girl's plight. Meanwhile, their leader readied his bow, plucking an arrow from his quiver, and waited for the right moment to reveal himself.

As he watched the battle unfold, he was disturbed to see the girl had sustained a long wound running from her right shoulder almost to her wrist. Hearing the rustle of his comrades coming up behind him, he carefully took aim at the goblin dueling the girl. With a soft twang from the bow, the arrow reached its mark sending mayhem among the goblins.

Again and again the bow thrummed, each time finding its target. From both sides of the dell, the dwarves swarmed in, hacking and driving the goblins back from the girl. The lead dwarf leapt from the top of the dell, landing beside her. Side by side, they attacked the goblins. The tide was now turned, and the dwarves made short work of the foul creatures.

Once the last goblin had been dispatched, the dwarven leader turned to the girl, noticing details about her for the first time. Her rich, chestnut colored hair was pulled back in a loose braid that fell to her waist. She had blue-gray eyes that were unreadable in the firelight. She wore a close fitting tunic and leggings in hues of dark greens and brown. Blood dripped down the guard of her sword from the wound on her arm. Both parties regarded each other in silence for a moment as they tried to catch their breath.

"Thank you," the girl said simply. "I didn't think I was going to make it out of that one."

"You're welcome," replied the leader of the dwarves. "If you don't mind me asking, who are you, and what are you doing out in the Wilds alone?"

"I am Avana. My business is my own, but since I owe you my life, I am willing to share my story with you," she said wearily. Upon seeing her fatigue, the dwarf gestured for her to sit down and the company of dwarves settled around the fire.

"You can call me Killian," the dwarf said. "We are traveling back home from trading gems along the Western Seas in the city of Tir Falken. We heard the sounds of fighting from the road. We were lucky to find you. May I see to your injury?"

"Yes, thank you. As you know, the goblins had me surrounded with my back to the fire and, as I attempted to fight through them, they got me," she regarded her wound with disgust. "Ruined my vambrace, but at least I still have an arm left!"

Killian let out a small chuckle at her ire as he pulled out a medical kit from his pack. "Are you hungry?" he asked.

"Unfortunately, yes," she said with a growl. "My stomach was my downfall. I was so tired of cold food that I decided to risk a fire in this dell. I hoped it would hide the light and smoke from anyone unpleasant, but that clearly failed."

"Well, we haven't eaten this evening yet either so I think we can whip something up," Killian smiled. "Patrick is a genius at finding fat rabbits."

The dwarves quickly and efficiently built up the fire and soon had a rabbit stew sizzling over the coals. Avana watched them distractedly, wincing when Killian pulled the vambrace off her arm in order to bandage the wound. A capable healer, he had in no time cleaned out the cut and was now carefully wrapping it.

Avana studied Killian as he finished bandaging her arm. He was tall for a dwarf and stood only a few inches shorter than her. He had dark hair that fell in wild twists to his shoulders, and dark eyes that danced with mischief. What struck Avana most was the unkempt scruff on his face. He lacked the full beard of the older dwarves with him, which told her he was easily the youngest in their group. Killian was handsome in a roguish way that spoke of a life rougher than his years. Despite his youth, Killian was clearly the leader, so Avana decided he must be someone important.

"You said you were heading home," Avana said. "Where is that for you?"

"The Cascade Mountains," Killian replied. "Under the great Tiered Mountain lies the

Dwarf Kingdom ruled by Halfor the Wise, who also happens to be my uncle. That's how I came to be in charge of this company. Halfor and I fought together in the Great War and, afterward, he gave me charge of all trading between the Mountain and the rest of Arda."

"So you are familiar with Amaroth, the city of Men," Avana said excitedly, as a bright light of interest lit up in her eyes. "That is where I am heading. Could I travel with your company there?"

"Yes," said Killian, in surprise, looking at her uncertainly. "But I must know why you wish to travel there."

Avana closed her eyes and sighed. "I suppose it is only right that I state my business. I am looking for my father."

"Your father?" Killian asked.

"Yes, my father," Avana said quietly. "Six years ago, I lived with my family on the edge of the Greenwood Forest. We lived off the land and had a small cabin in the woods. My father had been a Ranger, but after he lost his brother during the Great War with the goblins, he decided he no longer wanted to live that life. Instead, he married my mother and moved to the Forest. There they had three children and we lived happily. My father taught all three of us woodcraft and how to use a sword. I think a part of him had a Ranger's watchfulness that never ceased.

"One fateful day, my mother sent me down to the river to retrieve water for washing. It was a good distance from the cabin, and you couldn't see the building or hear the sounds of the family from the riverside. Like any other day, I dawdled along the bank, chasing frogs and playing with cattails. I disliked washdays and I always took as long as possible to get water. Normally I paid little attention to the forest behind me, but that day, I happened to look up as I snatched at a frog, the air smelling like something was burning. Then a billowing cloud of smoke drifted up from the direction of my home. In alarm, I raced back to the house. As I drew closer, I could hear the roar of flames; when I burst into the clearing, I was met with a terrible sight: the cabin I grew up in was ablaze. Raging flames leaped up toward the sky and the house was engulfed. The windows were shattered, and furniture was strewn about the ground outside the house. That was not the worst of it, however. I found my mother, sister, and brother all dead in front of the house. They were full of goblin arrows, and the ground around them held the tracks of dozens of the foul creatures. I was nearly hysterical with grief when I realized I had not seen my father with them. I frantically searched the clearing for his body. I didn't find it and foolishly began calling for him. I received no answer and, as I look back now, I am thankful the goblins did not hear me and return to kill me.

"I slowly began to have a small hope that my father was taken captive. I began to search diligently for signs of the goblins' path away from my home, and came upon a place where the ground was churned up mightily from a desperate battle. I recognized my father's footprints mingled with those of the goblins. Catching a glint of something in the sun, I noticed there, on the edge of the trees in the tall grass, was my father's great longsword. With trembling hands, I picked it up. This, to me, was proof that my father was a captive of the goblins. I was sure if they had killed him, I would have found him there. Why they took him I couldn't fathom, but I did know I had to try to find him. Eventually I picked up the goblins' trail and followed it. But the little knowledge I had of woodcraft didn't get me very far. I vowed that day I would never give up looking for my father—which brings me to today. I have been searching the Wilds for him ever since, until recently, when I received news that someone from Amaroth had seen my father. It was then I decided I should search for him there."

Killian studied her for a long moment, contemplating the tale Avana had told him. "Your story rings true. Your clothes are weather-stained from wandering. You are alone and there is obviously no one around for miles. I will choose to believe you," he said at last. "I am sorry for your loss. I, too, have lost a family member, my brother. He also died in the Great War. You said your father was a Ranger—what was his name? Also, is your grandfather still a Ranger?"

"My father's name is Caleb. My grandfather, Aramis, is indeed still a Ranger. He is the one who brought me the news pointing me to Amaroth," Avana said with a broken smile.

"Aramis is your grandfather? He's the head Ranger! Your family is a direct line from the kings who ruled the Wilds of old, before they became the desolation they are now. Are you aware of that?" Killian said incredulously. "Your father and his brother were heroes during the Great War. The elves sing epics about them!"

As Killian spoke, he watched astonishment cross Avana's face. For a moment she looked stunned, then she rallied and said, "I didn't know any of that . . . I knew Grandfather was the head Ranger, but didn't realize it was anything special. I suppose when my father left the Rangers, he wanted a completely different life. I think my mother must have known, but she never let on. Father never did like the spotlight, so I can see how being called a hero would make him want to hide. He always told us the war was a terrible thing, and he wished he could have his brother Cale back."

"They were very brave men, Avana," Killian said gently. "Your uncle gave his life to save many others, including you. I'm sure your father knew that."

"I just can't believe I never knew all this. I guess that's what happens when you have wandered alone for so long . . ." Avana spoke softly as she looked into the leaping flames.

"We don't normally invite strangers into our company. However, I am uncomfortable leaving you alone in the Wilds. We will take you to Amaroth, Avana. I hope Caleb is there and you can be reunited with him," said Killian with an air of hopeful finality.

At that moment another dwarf brought them each a bowl of rabbit stew and the company ate quietly. Afterwards they set up camp for the night.

Killian declared, "We'll each take four-hour shifts of watch tonight, in case any more goblins appear."

"Which shift is mine?" Avana asked.

"You're in no shape to be keeping watch. Rest tonight. You can take part other nights," Killian replied firmly.

Avana felt so drained after the attack that she decided not to press the matter. With a sigh, she walked off a few paces away from the dwarves and opened her pack. Killian noticed she pulled out a great white pelt. It had long shaggy fur that shone in the moonlight like silk. It was longer than Avana when she laid it out on the ground, and easily cocooned her when she pulled it around herself. It reminded Killian of the wolves he had seen along the mountain foothills. With a start, he realized that was exactly what the fur was from. This pelt was monstrous compared to those wolves. He wondered greatly where Avana had come by it. Killian decided he would ask her the next day and crawled into his own bedroll for the night.

Chapter 2

EARLY IN THE MORNING, THE COMPANY AWOKE and readied themselves. The sky was still dark when they left to hasten on their way. They traveled in silence until the sun began to peek over the horizon with a pink glow. Killian walked beside Avana as they marched along. He continued to study her as they went. She was constantly wary, yet she strode with a confidence belying her age. Her clothes were worn, and she wore a dark-colored cloak over lightweight leather armor.

"Last night, I saw you had a great white fur. How did you come by it? It looked like a wolf skin," queried Killian.

"It is," Avana answered slowly. "It was a gift from a friend. From the Wolves of the Far North." This was all she would say about the pelt and Killian sensed he would get no more out of her on the subject. Instead, Avana surprised him by asking about his bow. She plied him with questions about techniques and how archery compared to the use of other weapons.

Finally, Killian laughed and said, "Why don't you learn to shoot? I can teach you to use a bow much easier than answering all of your questions."

Avana looked at him sharply. "Do you really mean that?"

"Of course," Killian countered. "I think you would pick up archery quickly. It takes long hours of practice, but I imagine you could become competent between here and Amaroth."

"I believe I will take you up on your offer. I'll do anything I can do to destroy those filthy goblins. Besides, a bow can be used with more stealth than a sword. I can pick off the enemy from a distance and they would never know my exact location if I time it right," Avana replied.

"When we break for a meal I can begin to teach you," Killian smiled enthusiastically. He then went into detail on battle tactics with a bow and Avana listened intently as they journeyed onward. She continued to question him closely and Killian found that, despite her youth, Avana had a brilliant mind for strategy. She constantly analyzed the scenarios he put before her and was never satisfied with just one answer. Eventually, they stopped for their meal break.

Afterwards, Killian took one of the old bags that had carried jewels and stuffed it with heather. He set it up against a bush and paced off ten yards away from it. In one smooth motion he pulled an arrow from his quiver, nocked it, drew back, and shot. The arrow struck the center of the bag with a soft thwack and stuck partway out. This satisfied Killian. He did not wish his arrows to go through and be ruined. He called Avana over to him.

"I do not have a bow that will fit you properly, but I can teach you the basics with mine.

You are taller than I, but I think in wingspan we are similar. That is what will really affect you at first. My fear is the draw will be too heavy for you. I'm afraid all of our bows are the same. If you cannot pull mine back, then there is little I can teach you," Killian stated.

"Let us hope I have the strength then," Avana declared while removing her pack.

"When you draw a bow, you don't pull back. Instead, I want you to imagine yourself pulling it apart, the string from the wood. Try to make it one smooth motion. Dragging through it will make draw back much more difficult," Killian spoke patiently. "Stand with your feet shoulder width apart. Draw the bow, and bring the string to an anchor point. Most people find the corner of their mouth is best for them. The key is to always bring your hand back to the same spot when you draw. Relax your arms. Don't stiffen the arm holding the bow; let it float in your hand. Now, let's see you try the draw."

Hesitantly, Avana took the bow from Killian. The wood and its weight felt smooth and comfortable under her hand. She carefully took the stance Killian had outlined. With a deep breath, she pulled back the bow. Avana's muscles protested at the movement, but when she reached full draw, her body relaxed into the pull. It was not easy to hold the draw weight, but she found she could do it.

"Excellent," pronounced Killian. "Now look down the arrow, letting the arrow guide your eyes to the target, and aim for a spot on the bag. Let the arrow hover over it. Take steady breaths and when you feel ready, release the arrow on your exhale and leave your hand anchored at your face."

Avana did exactly as she was told; when she felt confident of her aim, she released the arrow. It hit the bag with a thwack only a few inches from Killian's arrow.

"I hit it!" She cried happily.

"Of course you did," Killian replied. "The bow does not miss easily when you handle it correctly. Try again. Aim for the same spot as before."

For the next few shots, Killian made minor adjustments to Avana's position, lifting her elbow a tad higher, straightening her frame, and helping her find the best balance. After a dozen shots, Avana grew tired and they quit their lesson for the day. Killian advised her to practice drawing back the bow ten times every evening to build up her arm strength.

Avana practiced shooting daily as they journeyed toward Amaroth. Killian continued to critique her and her skill with the bow improved.

Soon, a friendship was forged between the two. They walked together and often discussed battle strategy along with ways to hunt down goblins. This made the rest of the dwarves shake their heads. They also had grown to care for Avana, and it troubled them that she was so bent on revenge and searching for her father. Dwarves have few children, and Avana's liveliness and youth made them smile into their beards. She was endlessly curious about the lives of dwarves, knowing next to nothing about them.

Avana had led a sheltered life growing up in the Greenwood Forest. Even during her search for her father, she had avoided contact with almost everyone. Avana never tired of asking them questions, especially about their work with metal and jewels. In turn, she showed them new ways to stalk and hide themselves. She could disappear almost instantly, if she wished, and it was nearly impossible to track her. Killian often marveled at how easily she could hide, even in the open. Her cloak, in the Ranger's style, was a great aid to her because it allowed her to blend into her surroundings.

Avana regaled them with tales of sneaking into goblin tunnels in search of her father. She was looking for the slave holes, where goblins kept their prisoners for sport and hard labor.

"I was only able to free four men in all of my hunting," Avana regretfully said. "The goblins have their prisons too well fortified."

"I cannot believe you rescued anyone from those death holes," Killian announced in surprise. "One does not often walk into a goblins' nest and return alive. You are indeed not like others of your kind. Even an elf would think twice about searching a goblins' lair."

"I fear you are right, Killian. I'm not like my mother or sister. I wish only for battle and to see my father restored. I don't know if I will ever be able to fall in love or lead a life without danger. But this is the life I have chosen and I will not run from it," Avana said forlornly.

This disturbed Killian, causing him to turn away from her to hide his face. It wasn't right for a youth to carry such a burden. He vowed to himself to help her any way he could. Perhaps someday her feelings would change. After all, Avana was still very young and, with what she had gone through, he could understand her sentiments.

As Amaroth drew closer, Avana became very quiet, especially once they reached the main road leading to the city. When meeting other travelers along the path, she hesitated to return their greetings. As Avana and the dwarves made camp on the outskirts of the city, she confided her fears to Killian.

"I've never been around this many people before," she confessed. "They make me feel all scrunched up inside, like I haven't got any place to be myself. I know hardly anything about society, and I'm terribly afraid of getting things all wrong and muddled when I interact with others."

"You needn't worry," said Killian. "Most of these people look at you and they see a Ranger. Folks are a bit wary of Rangers, so they will leave you alone, and any strange mannerisms will be attributed to the Rangers. Don't go lording your adventures over people, but also don't allow them to intimidate you. You'll find they will show you kindness if you are open with them. Tomorrow we will enter the city. I will take you to the Commander of the Guard. If anyone has news of your father, it will be him."

Chapter 3

AVANA AWOKE EARLY THE NEXT MORNING and found herself gazing out at the countryside around her. First she looked upon the great rolling plains that disappeared into the Wilds. Her old life was there, with all its comfortable familiarity. Turning east, she looked to the city where she knew her future was. As the sun rose, it glistened off the imposing Cascade Mountains and the nearby Lonrach Lake, casting a dazzling glare like a gem. The radiance of the city's walls in the bright sun gave Avana a dose of courage. Surely a place as beautiful as this would hold answers about her father.

By now, the dwarves were awake and busy preparing to enter Amaroth. They repacked their belongings and pulled out money purses to buy trinkets for loved ones. Amaroth was the last leg of their journey and they were anxious to return home after their long absence. Avana was surprised to find they had not made any breakfast, but the dwarves smiled and told her it was their tradition to eat at the famous Highwater Inn when returning from a long journey.

When the city gates opened for the day, the company walked under the great stone arches, crafted to resemble two immense dragons whose necks curled and twined together. Avana marveled at the stonework for she had seen nothing like it before.

Killian noticed her gaping and laughed. "The arches are of dwarven make as a token of our friendship with men. However, they pale in comparison to the stone in the halls of Halfor! I wish someday you would look upon those halls with me."

"One day, perhaps I will!" said Avana, feeling abashed. "I see that I know very little about dwarves or men! I can't even tell the difference between their craftsmanship."

"To make it easier for you, generally, anything here made from wood was crafted by men, while anything of stone or precious gems the dwarves had a hand in making," Killian explained kindly. "And, if it's made of metal, your guess is as good as mine! The weaponry here comes from all peoples—dwarves, men, and elves. Most swords, though, are elf-made. Dwarves supply them with the steel, but the elves add something to make the blade even stronger."

"And what would that be?" Avana asked.

"Almost all the swords have spells woven in them, to make them last longer and give the user protection. But the named swords also have bright silver mixed with the steel, which makes them nearly unbreakable," Killian answered.

"I've never heard of bright silver. What is it?"

"Bright silver is a metal the elves created. Only they know the secrets to making it. It is extremely lightweight but cannot be broken unless brought to a forge. If bright silver is mixed with other metals, like steel, it enhances the metal, giving it the best of all of its qualities while improving the metal itself," Killian replied.

"And what exactly is a named sword?" Avana asked, looking perplexed.

"A named sword is one made specifically for a person or a purpose. It is given a name while it is being made and certain spells that go with the name are forged into it, giving the sword great power. Not many swords are made this way. Your uncle Cale had a very famous named sword, Darkbane, but it was lost in the War. It had power against those who wished him ill when he wielded it."

Avana spoke quickly, "Hang on a minute; I carry my father's sword. He never mentioned it had a name though. Is it possibly important?"

"Yes!" said Killian. "Let's look at it, but if it's the same one he had in the Great War, then it is indeed a named sword and even more famous than Darkbane."

Moving to the side of the street, they stopped. Avana unbuckled her sheath, slung the sword over her head, and held it out to Killian. He carefully pulled the blade partway out and examined it closely. Then, shaking his head in wonderment, he re-sheathed the sword and handed it back to Avana.

"That's it!" Killian cried out excitedly. "I can't believe I didn't recognize it before now. That's Stelenacht, the "Light in the Dark." If the bearer of the sword speaks its name over it, the sword will glow with a blue light until it is sheathed. It's said the light can cut through the darkest night and put fear into the heart of the goblins. That sword is worth more than your life. Its fame is known throughout the entire continent of Arda! Do not let people know what blade you carry. Cover the markings, and you will be safe."

"Again, I am amazed at what I find out about my father," Avana replied, feeling a mix of curiosity and frustration. "I know more about him now that he's gone than I did before the goblins captured him. I feel as though I am putting together a puzzle, whose pieces I must search for as I go along."

"Indeed it seems that way," Killian agreed, looking her over in a new light. "Now that you know the sword's name, it will be a great boon for you in battle. Come! Let us hurry on into the city. Perhaps the Commander of the Guard will have another piece for your puzzle."

They hurried on, winding up and down the streets, until they were near the heart of the city. There, a large rectangle was walled off, and inside the walls, lay the city's barracks and training grounds for the highly skilled warriors of Amaroth. The Commander of the Guard often had dealings with dwarves from Halfor's kingdom, thus they were quickly granted access to his office.

The city of Amaroth did not have a king, but was instead ruled by a group of Elders, one from each part of the city's main districts. There were seven total, which included the Commander of the Guard as Amaroth's army was considered its own district. This put the commander in a position to access much knowledge of the comings and goings of the city and the lands around Amaroth. If anyone had possible information about Avana's father, it would be him.

Killian and Avana waited patiently outside the commander's office. Soon they heard a deep voice bidding them to enter. They pushed open the weighty door and walked into a sparsely furnished room. A heavy, dark wood desk took center stage, and a painting depicting mountains and several swords were the only decorations on the walls. A tall, lithe man with dark, silver-laced hair stood behind the desk. He was clothed in the dark red of the Guard with a gold dragon emblazoned on his chest. He looked at the visitors with appraising steel-blue eyes.

"Welcome," he said simply. "My name is Ruskin, Commander of the Guard of the city of Amaroth. What brings you to my office?"

Killian stepped forward and spoke. "My name is Killian, son of Kalmar, brother of Halfor, King under the Tiered Mountain. My companion is Avana of the Wilds, daughter of the Ranger

Caleb, and granddaughter of Aramis, head of the Rangers. She comes to you seeking news of her father, who was abducted by a war party of goblins."

"Daughter of Caleb," Ruskin said in astonishment. "We had heard news that your family was attacked. I did not realize anyone survived. You bring me great joy with this news if it is true. But how do I know you are really who you say you are?"

"I carry my father's sword, Stelenacht," Avana said, and with a swift motion pulled the sword from its sheath. The sword's edges glimmered a soft blue, giving the blade a deadly look.

A sharp intake of breath was briefly the only sign Ruskin gave as he gazed at the glowing blade. "I know this sword. It is indeed Caleb's. You stand like him, and you carry the blade in the style he preferred. Indeed, you must be his daughter," he said at long last. "Please, tell me your story. Why didn't Aramis say anything to me about this, I wonder . . ." This last comment was said almost to himself as Ruskin settled into a chair. "Sit. Make yourselves comfortable."

With that, Avana and Killian sat across from the commander, and Avana recounted her tale to him. As she talked, Ruskin questioned her closely on a variety of details. He wanted to know things like the exact time of day when the goblins attacked, and other parts of her story. When Avana glossed over how she survived in the Wilds so well on her own, Ruskin got a peculiar glint in his eyes, clearly guessing more about her story than what she would say. Finally, after having her repeat the story, he sat back in his chair.

"One thing bothers me about your tale. How is it your grand-father has not been taking care of you? Aramis has always been protective of his family," Ruskin said.

"Because he is a Ranger, I didn't think I could find him to contact him. Unfortunately, I never found out where the Ranger

base was when I was young—Grandfather always came to us
to visit after my grandmother, Ruth, passed away. I knew the
Rangers travel all throughout the land, rarely staying in one place
for long. It happened by chance that I came across his camp in
the Wilds. He's the one who told me to come to Amaroth. He
had news that a former Ranger was a prisoner of the goblins, and
this information had come from here. Grandfather wanted me
to stay with him, but I refused. I intend to continue searching
for my father," Avana said stubbornly.

"So Aramis let you go," Ruskin said thoughtfully. "He must
trust you if he allowed you to continue your search. You are very
young, but you seem to have wisdom and skill beyond your years.
You have come to the right place, Avana. Indeed there has been
news of a Ranger taken captive. I did not realize it was your
father, however. There are many retired Rangers in the land."

A light kindled in Avana's eyes as he spoke. She leaned forward
eagerly, "What can you tell me? And how old are the tidings?"

"Very little, I'm afraid," Ruskin said with a wry smile. "About
three months ago, we heard news that a man was rescued from
the Wilds. He was part of a group of goblin prisoners being
transferred to another goblin tribe. He somehow managed to
escape when they were above ground. He mentioned a former
Ranger was in his group and had helped him to escape thanks
to his knowledge of the goblins. He wanted to go back to
rescue the other prisoners but didn't know where the goblins
had taken them."

Breathlessly Avana asked, "What was the man's name? Where
might I find him? How soon do you think I could meet him?"

"Ah, that is where the dilemma lies. I'm sorry to say I was
never given his name, and as to where he now lives, I do not
know. I can, however, send you to the man who found him. He
is a captain of an outpost we keep on the edge of the Wilds,"

Ruskin said. "The location is a close secret we share only with the Rangers because we do not want the goblins to find it. The captain, whose name is Marco, usually returns a few times a year on leave. His next scheduled return is coming up. I can arrange a meeting for you then."

Avana sat back in her chair to digest all the information Ruskin had given her. After a moment she again spoke. "Commander, you have given me great hope and much to think about. I cannot thank you enough for the information you provided! I will do as you say and wait for the captain's return. When do you expect him?"

Ruskin smiled. "He should be here by the end of next week, provided his travels go well. I will set up a meeting for you as soon as possible."

"Again, thank you for your kindness. I am greatly indebted to you," Avana said happily. "Is there anything I can do to repay you?"

"Perhaps, but it would be much greater than the worth of a meeting and some information. Your experiences intrigue me, as do your skills. The Guard is always looking for highly skilled trackers, and your knowledge of the Wilds is invaluable. Would you consider joining the Guard of Amaroth?" Ruskin asked. "I would send you on missions to places far away so you could continue to search for your father while soldiering."

"I don't know . . . may I have a day to think about your offer? All of this is so very new to me that I don't wish to jump into anything hastily," Avana answered cautiously.

"Yes, it's a serious decision. Commitment to the Guard is a minimum of three years so I would not want you to take your choice lightly," Ruskin replied.

"Then I shall come back to you tomorrow with my answer," Avana said with a smile. "There is much for me to take in, but I promise I will not make light of your request."

With that, Avana and Killian took their leave from the Commander and walked back out to the city square.

Killian spoke first. "I am happy for you, Avana. You have a real lead toward finding your father. And you have a job offer. It's not easy to become part of the Guard of Amaroth. I know you said you wanted to think about it overnight, but what is your first reaction? Will you take him up on his offer?"

"Indeed, it is very fortunate I was able to hear this news. I have a starting place now for my search. As for Commander Ruskin's proposal, I'm not sure yet. I suppose my gut says to take the opportunity, but my head isn't so sure I want to lose all my freedoms," Avana said thoughtfully.

"I can understand that," Killian said gently. "Becoming part of the Guard would be very different for you."

"I suppose I should say *yes*. Being a member of the Guard would be an excellent way to hear information, and I would have more resources to help me find my father," Avana said.

Killian studied her for a long moment. "I think becoming part of the Guard would be a good fit for you. I cannot see you working in some seamstress shop or other such employment. You are brave, wily in the ways of woodcraft, and an excellent strategist. You need more purpose to your life, and here is an excellent opportunity."

"Then I suppose I should take it," Avana said. "Now that the matter is settled, I wonder what this Captain Marco will have to say. I hope he can give me more than the man's name."

"I will wait with you until you are able to meet him. Normally, I would go on to my home, but I would like to help you search for your father as much as I can. I will send the rest of the dwarves onward with the message that I will follow shortly," Killian said with finality.

Avana looked at him gratefully, "You would stay with me?"

"Of course," Killian exclaimed. "Am I not your friend? It is not the way of a dwarf to leave a friend in need."

Avana's heart swelled with gratitude at Killian's words, and she felt immensely relieved. She realized she had dreaded her parting with Killian. He was her first real friend in a long time. Although it was simply postponing the inevitable, Avana was comforted that he would stay a while longer, especially as she was meeting the strange Captain Marco.

"I find myself again indebted to you. Thank you for staying," Avana said. Her eyes shone happily as she spoke, causing Killian's heart to leap within him and catching him off guard. They turned and walked on, deeper into the city, deliberating the possibilities of meeting the captain. As they wandered through the market, Avana walked slowly past each stall, marveling at all of the trinkets and quality wares the citizens were selling. Beautiful swaths of cloth, finer than anything she had ever seen, fluttered in the breeze, while small delicately made toys fascinated her as they sat in tidy rows along a bench. There was also dainty jewelry laid out cleverly to catch the glint of sunshine, causing them to sparkle brightly. One necklace in particular caught her eye. It had a simple silver chain, but the pendant was a delicately wrought star with a gleaming diamond set in the center.

Avana couldn't help herself; she walked over to the necklace and gently traced the outline of the pendant. The seller eyed her eagerly and began rattling off the values of the necklace. Killian had watched Avana intently as she took in all of the market's spectacles. He noticed how she jerked in surprise and began to back away when the jewelry seller named the price. On a sudden impulse, Killian approached the vendor and said, "I'll buy that necklace." The seller nodded with a greedy smile as Avana mumbled behind Killian that he had no need to do such a thing. As he paid for the necklace, he thought how strange it was for him, as a dwarf, to have such familiarity with a human. Holding the necklace out to Avana, he declared, "Let this be a gift to symbolize our friendship between man and dwarf. May I put it on you?"

Looking quite bashful and uncertain, Avana nodded her assent. Stepping behind Avana, Killian carefully drew the chain around her neck brushing aside her long hair to fasten it.

"There," he said contentedly. "Now you really look the part of Caleb's daughter. Aramis could give you nothing finer. You come from royal blood, Avana. It's time you looked it!"

"But I am nothing but a wanderer bent on rescue and revenge. This seems much too refined for me," Avana protested with wide eyes.

Killian stilled her. "Nonsense. Accept your birthright. I too may prefer my travel clothes to frippery, but it doesn't mean I reject who I am. Take pride in your heritage. And if you struggle with that, then can you at least accept it as a gift from a friend?"

"I think I can do that," Avana beamed as she fingered the lovely pendant. "Thank you! Perhaps someday, when my quest is over, I can somehow repay you for your kindness."

Killian waved her thanks away as they walked through the market and proceeded back to the Highwater Inn.

CHAPTER 4

THE NEXT DAY AVANA WENT BACK to the Commander of the Guard to inform him of her decision. Ruskin was delighted, as Killian had suspected he would be. Instead of following the normal policy of starting training immediately, Ruskin allowed Avana a grace period until she could speak to Captain Marco. She was already extremely competent in most weaponry, so he planned to place her on an accelerated track when she did begin training. Although he did not tell Avana, he fully expected her to rise to the position of captain in just a year's time.

The following week flew by quickly for Avana; she thoroughly explored Amaroth while waiting for Captain Marco. She was fitted for a uniform and armor of the Guard. Avana relished showing off her new armor to Killian who enjoyed her excitement over the battle gear.

Avana admired this new turn of events with delight. "I've never had armor this well-made or fitting so nicely. This is most excellent!"

She was careful to slowly ease into wearing her new gear, but after two days, she was ready for some real action in it. Avana eagerly invited Killian to spar with her. They spent several hours doing just that one afternoon as she adjusted to fighting in her armor. It was a bit heavier than what she was used to, shifting on her body differently than she had expected. Nonetheless, Avana was not worried. She knew it wouldn't take long to become accustomed to the changes.

Finally, news of Captain Marco's return reached them. He was to stay in Amaroth for nearly a month before returning to his post. This would give Avana ample time to find out all she could from him. True to his word, Commander Ruskin quickly arranged a time for Avana and Killian to meet Marco. When the day of the meeting arrived, Avana felt like a bundle of nerves. So much was at stake from just a simple meeting! She knew it was a desperately slim hope this was really her father Captain Marco heard about, but she had to hope. Avana was driven to continue searching for her father, or wreak havoc and revenge on the goblins if he was dead.

A wet, cool morning dawned the day of the meeting. Avana shivered from the chilly air and her nerves as she and Killian headed to the barracks. Neither of them had much to say as they walked across the city. Time would soon give them plenty to talk about.

They entered the barracks and quickly made their way to the side office where Captain Marco was waiting to meet them. The captain was a bear of a man, but of average height. He had shaggy brown hair and a craggy face with deep brown eyes peering from it. His eyes carried a wild gleam in them, causing his observers to wonder if he was going to charge them or bellow out a strict order. Instead, he did neither, and engulfed each of them in a hearty handshake, his massive form swallowing even Killian, who was not a small dwarf.

"Glad to finally meet you," Marco voiced in a rough burr. "The commander filled me in on your quest and I'm happy to be of service if I can."

"Likewise, it is a pleasure to meet you, Captain," Avana said respectfully.

"Ach! Call me Marco. Forget the formality. We've got more important things to attend than that," Marco answered vigorously.

"Well then, Marco, what can you tell us about the man you rescued?" Avana asked anxiously.

"Not as much as you would probably like, I'm afraid. I can give you his name though. His name is Jare Sanger. He lives by the Western Seas now. He wanted to get as far away from the Wilds as he could after we rescued him," Marco replied.

"It's no surprise after the time he must have had," Killian nodded in sympathy.

Marco began, "I can tell you the name of town where I last heard he was living, but I don't know if he's still there. We really didn't have much contact with him after we helped him recover from his ordeal. Our last point of contact was in a town called Mahir, a small fishing village on the shore. I'm sorry I can't give you more than that. I do know for sure it was a Ranger who helped Jare to escape, but I never heard the name of the man."

"This at least gives me a fairly good idea of where to find him," Avana responded. "The only trouble is I don't know how I will manage to trek all the way to the Western Sea as I have just enlisted in the Guard."

"That part is easy," Killian answered, smiling at the pair. "I will find him. I make several trips a year to the Western Seas to trade. It would be simple for me to detour a bit on the road."

"Really? You would do that for me?" Avana asked in hopeful surprise.

Killian replied indignantly, "Well, *of course* I would. You've already thoroughly piqued my interest in the whole matter. I feel like I have a personal stake in this. I want to help find your father. No one deserves to be a goblin slave, least of all a Ranger. Do *not* doubt the loyalty of a dwarf!"

Marco laughed heartily at the exchange and shook his head with a smile. "Don't underestimate a dwarf, lass. They may be stubborn, but they rarely fail you. You should accept his proposition."

"I'm sorry, Killian," Avana said. "It's still a bit hard to get used to the idea that I don't have to do everything on my own."

"All is forgiven, Avana," Killian answered, smiling roguishly, "as long as you promise to make me a venison stew before I leave that's as good as the one you made the other day."

With a hearty laugh and exaggerated sigh, Avana said, "I *suppose* it could be arranged."

Smiling broadly, Marco said, "This pleases me greatly. I hope you can find Jare in Mahir. He's got sandy blond hair and an average build. What stands out about him the most are his eyes. They are the brightest green I've ever seen. Can't hide them. That's about all the description I can give you."

Killian looked thoughtful. "That's enough for me to go on, I believe. Besides, not many people out there have escaped from the goblins. I'm guessing everyone in the area will know him just from his past."

"Is there anything else you can tell us, Marco?" Avana asked. "I don't want to take up any more of your time than necessary. You have already been so kind to meet with us."

"Ah, lassie, I don't have anything else to say about Jare. That's all I know. And you have not been a bother in the least. A soldier's first job is to help others and this is how I can help you. I wish I could lead you straight to the hole where those miserable creatures are keeping your father, but sadly, I don't have that information," Marco said with an air of seriousness.

Avana paused for a moment to contemplate this new piece to her father's puzzle then lifted her gaze to Marco's face. "Thank you for your time and the information you gave us. It seems now I have a real chance to rescue my father. I intend to find him, even if I have to go through every goblin lair in the Wilds to do so!"

"I don't doubt you would," Marco answered, a respectful look dawning in his eyes. "It's been a pleasure to meet the two of you, and I hope you find him. Let me know if you do. Caleb and Cale were good men."

"Certainly!" Avana promptly replied. "It would give me great pleasure."

With that the two parties bid each other farewell. As they walked away from the barracks back to the Highwater Inn, Avana quietly asked Killian without looking up, "So when do you plan to leave?"

Killian hesitated, not wanting to continue. "Day after tomorrow would be best," he said at last.

"I've kept you too long here anyway," Avana replied, pointedly not looking at him.

"No, a missing Ranger is a serious matter. Halfor would want me to help you," said Killian quickly. "But the sooner I get back, the sooner I can start off again and search for this man Jare."

Avana shuffled her feet and looked troubled. "I know, but I am going to miss you. You're my first friend in a very long time."

"I shall miss you too," Killian responded. "It's not every day I find a strange girl in the Wilds on my journeys. If you wouldn't mind, I would like to write to you of my adventures and findings. I hope you don't think it too forward of me," he said with a wink.

Avana laughed and waved at him as if to shoo away the impertinence. "I really don't care what people think! How am I supposed to hear what you find otherwise? Correspondence with you will help me adjust by having someone to tell my experiences to."

"Then it's settled. Almost every town has message riders. I will update you when I reach Mahir. Although, I'm afraid it may be several months before I will have another expedition for trading along the Western Seas," Killian replied.

"Don't worry. It's enough knowing you'll go when you can. I'll have something to look forward to, rather than waiting until you pass through Amaroth again."

They retired that night to the Highwater Inn, and spent the next day preparing for Killian's journey while trying to make the most of their few hours together. When the day was spent, they invited Marco to enjoy a meal with them at the Inn. They applauded his tales from the Wilds, talking late into the night.

The time came for Killian's departure at dawn the following morning. Both struggled to say their goodbyes. They stood at the city gates. Killian had his bow slung over his shoulder and a sturdy pack on his back. Avana was stormy-eyed and wrestled with everything she wanted to tell him. Finally, she settled on simply saying, "Goodbye, my friend, and thank you for all you have done!" She looked directly into Killian's eyes as she spoke.

Killian, too, was torn and searched for the right words. "Goodbye, Avana. I will write to you. I hope to return soon with news of Caleb." He turned to leave but paused momentarily. Looking back at Avana, he swung around again, took a step forward and embraced her.

Without words, Avana hugged him back fiercely. Then they parted, and without a backward glance, Killian marched down the road. Avana watched him go until he was out of sight. With blurry eyes and a heavy heart, she headed for the barracks where her training would begin. She reported to the office headquarters and was given her room number. She was to share a room with another of the female recruits and felt anxious to meet her. Avana walked down the hallway searching for room 315. Arriving at the door, she found the chamber already occupied by her new roommate.

The girl inside turned to greet her, calling out, "Hullo! I assume you're my new roomie? I'm Nora, by the way! I hope you don't mind I took the bed closest to the door. You get the window bed. Sleeping next to the window gives me the chills."

A startled look crossed Avana's face as she took in the girl's torrent of details. Avana was normally not much of a talker, and Nora had said more in the span of a few seconds than Avana often did in a few hours.

She quickly shot a shy smile at Nora after introducing herself. "I don't mind the widow at all. Cold doesn't bother me." Avana spoke softly as she studied Nora, who was about her height, but there the similarities ended. Nora had dark brown hair and laughing brown eyes. Whereas Avana was lean and catlike, Nora was broad, built like a solid oak. Without missing a beat, Nora launched into another topic.

"I heard you have been wandering around alone for ten years or something like that! And you traveled with dwarves. What were they like? Have an eye on any of the other recruits yet?" Nora chattered, finally pausing for a breath.

Nora's stream of questions caused Avana to feel a bit taken aback, but the last comment made her giggle. "I was only alone for six years, and I wasn't just wandering. I was searching for my father, who was captured by goblins. Yes, I traveled with dwarves. They brought me to Amaroth. They are very stubborn and sometimes a bit rude, but truly very sweet and loyal. I miss them, honestly. As for the other recruits, I suppose I'm not really interested. I really want to find my father more than anything right now," Avana replied. She surprised herself with how much she had shared.

"Pretty much everyone has heard about your father now," Nora answered thoughtfully. "I'm really sorry that happened to him . . . and you! I intend to flirt with all the men enlisted in our class! Maybe one of them will turn out to be what I'm looking for."

Avana's shock must have shown on her face because Nora laughed heartily for a moment. "You should see your face! I won't really flirt with all of them. I just like to have big goals—and handsome guys! Although, I doubt we will get much chance to do anything fun until after the first three months are over. We train almost straight through and then get a break before being assigned."

Avana walked over to her bed and plopped her pack down. "Do you know what our training entails?"

"Lots of drills with different weapons, horseback riding, swimming, strategic planning, and a course on woodcraft, which basically means they teach us to be sneaky," Nora said, rolling her eyes. "With some of the sods I've met already, those instructors are going to have a tough time."

Grinning broadly, Avana said, "I can be pretty sneaky. I can't wait for that course!"

Nora sighed. "Well, it's the last course before they send us out, so I'm afraid you will have a while to wait."

"Too bad," Avana said, frowning.

"All the fun stuff they save for the end. Archery and swimming are my thing. We don't work on those until later either. I'm the best swimmer in all of Amaroth. I won the race across Lonrach two years in a row, but we won't get to swim until the second month."

"That's really neat. I can survive in the water, but my swimming definitely could be improved," Avana replied.

"I can help you out. After everything I have heard about you, I bet you will improve quickly," Nora assured.

They continued to chat as they set up the small room to their liking. It had just enough room for the two beds and two wooden chests. Avana noticed Nora had tied back the window curtains with a bright blue ribbon in a jaunty bow. With a pang Avana realized it reminded her of her mother, and the cabin she grew up in. They spent the rest of the day roaming the halls of the barracks, meeting the other new recruits.

Chapter 5

BREAKFAST WAS AT 6:00 SHARP THE NEXT MORNING, with roll call directly after. Avana had no trouble waking, but had to shake Nora, who slumbered on even after the wake-up bell. Breakfast consisted of eggs and a thick slice of warm sourdough bread. Gray clad recruits lined the hall as the sun peeked over the horizon. At 6:40, the bell rang again and they were led to the granite courtyard and lined up for inspection. Here they were split into groups of ten, then ushered to various alcoves of the yard. Nora and Avana were in the same group, for which Avana was grateful.

Their trainer and captain for the next three months was Grayson Hale, a half-breed. *His mother was a dwarf and his father a man,* Avana heard one of the other recruits whisper. He also said Grayson was much older than most of the soldiers, probably in his late sixties, but he was one of the best around. Avana noticed his grace and perfect posture. As they filed into the alcove, Grayson had his back to them and turned only when he heard their footsteps. He was man height but much broader than any normal human. He also had a full beard, weathered gray by hard years, which fell nearly to his waist. His gray-green eyes roved over the recruits, but stopped with a look of staggered shock when they came to Avana.

"Aileen?" he exclaimed softly in a deep voice. "But surely not!"

"Aileen was my mother," Avana stammered, feeling uncomfortable being singled out. "My name is Avana."

Understanding dawned over Grayson's face. "Yes, I see it now. You are your mother's daughter. You look just like her. But your eyes are all Caleb's. And your bearing is more akin to him than to her. Forgive me! I knew your parents long ago."

Without further explanation, he turned back to focus on the rest of the group who were all staring with interest at the two of them.

"Recruits, today is a new day for you. For the next three months, you will train to be a soldier of the Guard. It won't be easy. I don't babysit, and if I catch you slacking, you'll wish you hadn't! Some of you will quit. There's no shame in that. Soldiering is difficult, and I would rather fight beside someone knowing they want to be with me than not. Any questions?"

The recruits were silent as they waited for Grayson's next words. "Right then, you may refer to me as Captain Grayson. Among yourselves, others, and the rest of the recruits you will only be called by your first name. You won't receive the title of soldier and your red uniforms until your three months of training are up. Is that clear?"

"Yes, Captain Grayson!" the group chorused, and with that, their training officially had begun.

Weapons, coupled with horseback riding, were first on the training agenda. Over the next several days, Avana easily fell into the routine. She often wondered about Captain Grayson's words from the first day, but wasn't comfortable approaching him about it. A week later he was the one to broach the subject. While working with her individually on knife throwing, Grayson suddenly asked, "Did your parents ever mention their lives before living in the Greenwood?"

"Not really," Avana replied, startled. "I think everything

that happened during the War caused them to leave their old lives behind."

Captain Grayson looked weary for a moment, and then replied, "Yes, I suppose that would make sense. Did they ever mention me by any chance?"

Avana shook her head, "I don't remember them saying your name, but they could have and I forgot! I've had sort of a lot happen since then . . ." she trailed off.

"Would it surprise you to hear that I knew them very well?" Grayson asked.

"No. I know my mother was from a village along Lonrach Lake near here. Her family raised horses for the Guard. My parents met because my father bought a horse from my mother's family. They rarely talked about those times, though. There's much I don't know about them so I would be very interested in anything you could tell me," Avana replied eagerly.

Grayson let out a great sigh and slowly answered Avana, "Well, to tell you the truth, I'm your uncle—half uncle, to be exact. My father first fell in love with a dwarf maid. She died during my birth. When my father remarried, he raised me with your mother—his child with my stepmother. Your mother and I are just two years apart. I didn't know your parents had any children. It's been that long since I've seen them. Although, I guess it's too late now for me to see Aileen."

This frank admission shocked Avana. She was astonished again by what she learned about her family. "Why did they never tell me about you?" she asked in frustration.

"We had a terrible fight. I didn't think Caleb should retire from being a Ranger. I believed he should have taken command of Amaroth as his birthright allows. Neither he nor Aileen wanted any of it though. We parted in anger and they left soon after," Grayson said sadly. "I have regretted that fight ever since.

I hope I can somehow make amends for my transgressions by helping you."

Avana felt for Grayson, even as she struggled with how to react to this new piece of family history. "Will you help me find my father?" she asked after a few long moments.

Grayson eyed her seriously. "I will do everything in my power to do so. Caleb was my friend, and I would like a chance to apologize for my words. I know this has been a great shock for you, and I'm sorry for not telling you sooner. I guess I was trying to find the right words."

"So you really are my uncle then, aren't you?" was Avana's quiet response.

"Yes, I am," Grayson smiled. "Though, I don't think you should go around telling people. They might accuse me of special treatment during training. I honestly didn't know you would be assigned to me. Commander Ruskin knows our connection. He's a good man and won't make a fuss over it. In fact, I wonder if he had a hand in you ending up in my group. That would be like him."

For the rest of the training session, the two talked about their pasts. Grayson was clearly apprehensive about Avana's abilities to survive in the Wilds on her own. But he let it go, knowing eventually she would tell him if she trusted him enough.

At the end of the first two weeks of training, pay was given to the recruits and a chart of their progress was posted. Avana was delighted to find her name at the top of the list. She had excelled in everything they had worked on, from archery to hand-to-hand combat. She silently thanked her years in the Wilds for her good marks, and thought wistfully of Killian when she saw her high numbers in archery. Her lowest score was in knives, and she was determined to improve that.

An idea in her head, she hesitantly walked over to Captain

Grayson's quarters. After a moment of indecision, she knocked on his door. He answered and smiled merrily down at her.

"What brings you to my door, Avana?"

"I would like some help with something . . . Uncle," she stumbled over the name but continued hurriedly. "I want to buy some Saxe knives for throwing and close quarters fighting. I need more practice with them, and I think I will find them very useful. I just don't have any knowledge of what I should purchase," she finished.

Grayson's smile widened. "I am glad to hear you call me 'Uncle.' And I would be honored to help you find some knives that are right for you. We can go now if you like. Meet me in ten minutes at the courtyard doorway."

Avana hurried back to her room to retrieve her small money-bag and tied it to her belt. She also grabbed her father's sword, slinging it across her back and covering both the sword and money with her cloak. She paused for a moment to consider the sword the Guard had issued her but she didn't feel the need to carry two weapons. With that she practically flew to the courtyard where she met Grayson already in the doorway. He nodded approvingly at her attire as they began to walk swiftly to the market.

When they reached the weapons merchants they pored over dozens of knives until they found a pair that met Grayson's standards. The hilts were bound in plain black leather for the best possible grip, while the blades themselves were made from bright silver. They came with sturdy sheaths that easily hid beneath Avana's cloak. She eagerly paid the seller and tucked the knives into her belt. The pair wandered about the city for the rest of the morning before settling down under a shady tree to enjoy a lunch of bread and meat they'd just purchased.

Out of the blue, Grayson asked Avana, "I heard you carry

Caleb's sword. Do you also by any chance have a wolf skin with you?"

"Yes," Avana answered slowly. "I have a wolf pelt I used as a bedroll. How did you know?"

Instead of answering the question, Grayson recited in a low voice:

From the Wilds an heir will arise,
A wolf's coat the one will bear
And a sword of great deeds and dare,
The heir will unite the races
Against a common foe,
And when the war is over
A king again shall rule

Feeling confused by Grayson's strange reply, Avana asked, "What does that mean? Uncle, what are you not telling me?"

"Avana, I believe you are part of the prophecy. You are a direct descendant of the kings of old. You carry a very famous sword, and you keep a wolf skin. I believe you are the beginning of great changes to all the lands," Grayson alleged in a hushed tone. "That poem was given after the fall of the kingdom as a promise the king would rise again one day."

"But how would I unite men, dwarves, and elves? And what is our common foe?" Avana was more confused than she had ever been, and utterly annoyed, yet again, by her lack of knowledge of the common world.

Grayson replied gravely, "I don't know, Avana, but you're the first person in nearly five hundred years to fit the description of the prophecy."

"This is all too much! I don't understand any of it!" Avana protested.

Grayson appeared troubled for a moment, and then closing

his eyes, leaned back against the tree trunk. "Avana, you don't have to understand it, but I truly believe you are part of the prophecy. If it bothers you, then don't think about it! Live on as you are. If you are meant to fulfill it, then you will do so."

Avana pulled her knees up to her chest, hugging them. Her head swam with everything she had learned recently. First, she received credible news that her father might possibly still be alive; second, she found out she was from a direct line of royalty and carried a famous sword; and, third, she learned she had an uncle, and now she could be the answer to some age old prophecy? It was too much for her to absorb. She desperately wished Killian were here with her to help make sense of it all.

"Uncle Grayson? I think I would like to go back now. I need some time to consider all of this," Avana murmured after several minutes of silence.

Grayson nodded with a knowing gaze and kept quiet all the way back to the barracks. He bid her goodbye at the courtyard and watched her with concern as she headed to her room. Upon arrival, Avana was delighted to see a letter on the foot of her bed. She hastily tore open the heavy envelope and pulled out a letter written on a fine white page. It was from Killian, and for a short while, she forgot all of her concerns as she read his words.

Dear Avana,

I trust this letter finds you well. My journey home was uneventful and I made good time. I immediately went to see my uncle, Halfor, concerning your father and about arranging another expedition to the Western Seas. He knew your father and fought beside him in the War. He has granted me leave to help you find your father however I see fit. Halfor has arranged to have a trading expedition leave at the end of the month. It takes a little less than a month to travel to the Western Seas. I will be going with them, so I hope, in that time frame, I will acquire some sort of information as to your father's whereabouts.

Halfor mentioned something to me I should have remembered before. We believe you are part of a prophecy. If you haven't heard it, this is how it goes: "From the Wilds an heir will arise, a wolf's coat the one will bear and a sword of great deeds and dare, the heir will unite the races against a common foe, and when the war is over a king again shall rule." I realize that may seem foolish to you, but you perfectly match the description. Halfor, at least, is convinced you are the heir. He said to urge you not to announce that you match the prophecy's description until it has been fulfilled. Don't let your fellow soldiers know, at least.

How is training progressing? I will be coming through Amaroth in a few weeks' time, so I would suggest not sending a return letter for I fear I won't receive it. I'm sorry for the strange message. I look forward to seeing you again.

Your faithful friend,
Killian

For the second time that day, Avana was stunned. However, she was starting to feel more comfortable with everything she had learned. Clearly something much bigger than her was at work, but it wouldn't do to worry about it. Grayson had told her to put it aside and continue her life. In that moment, Avana decided that was exactly what she would do. She would train harder and work more diligently than ever. If that brought about the fulfillment of the so-called prophecy, so be it. And if not, she would have no regrets.

CHAPTER 6

AS THE MONTH WORE ON, Avana threw herself into training while impatiently awaiting Killian's arrival. She continued to score well on the testing even as the drills grew more difficult. She learned to refine her sword stroke and how to accurately shoot her bow while riding a running horse. Avana also practiced constantly with her new knives, not only with throwing them, but hiding them on her person.

One hot afternoon she stood on the archery course and carefully took aim at a target many paces away. Before she could release the arrow, she felt a hand on her shoulder. Without letting this gesture startle her, she let fly the arrow and looked on in satisfaction as it made a perfect target hit.

"Excellent shot!" a familiar voice quipped from behind her.

Avana spun around in delight and was lifted off her feet in a bear hug from Killian.

"You're finally here!" she exclaimed breathlessly as he set her down.

Killian grinned. "I couldn't keep a highborn lady like you waiting. That wouldn't be fitting."

"Oh, you're as full of yourself as ever," Avana laughed, as she took in the sight of him. He was more handsome than before, if that was possible. He was clad in fine dark leather that accented his eyes and made them glint with even more mischief than usual. Averting her gaze, she instead set her bow aside. "Come with me. There is someone I want you to meet," she announced.

"Of course," Killian replied, striding alongside her. As they advanced through the compound, he filled her in on his journey so far, and his plans to find Jare Sanger. Avana soon found who she was looking for in the hand-to-hand combat arena. Captain Grayson Hale stood on the sidelines, roaring out directions to two of the recruits from Avana's unit. When he saw Avana and Killian, he ordered the sparring pair to break for the day, muttering to himself as he so often did about incompetent soldiers.

"You must be Killian!" boomed Grayson, warmly shaking his hand. "You don't know it but I come from some of your kin. Halfor's second cousin's daughter was my mother. My name is Captain Grayson Hale. I am the uncle of young Avana here."

Killian's face registered a look of surprise that quickly changed to understanding. "You're Aileen's brother. I have heard about you but never knew your name. I am pleased to meet you. I am glad to find Avana has a friend here."

The two men engaged in an animated conversation about their ancestry and battles fought by their long dead family members. Avana wondered what she got herself into by bringing them together. Finally, their talk slowed and Grayson asked, "When do you continue your journey?"

"Tomorrow morning, I'm afraid," Killian replied.

"So soon?" Avana asked, trying to hide her disappointment.

"If I am going to search for Jare and complete my trading, I can stay no longer. I am sorry. I would have liked to stay for a while," said Killian with a sad air. "However, I intend to make the most of my time today. May I take you and Captain Grayson out to dinner this evening? With your permission, sir."

Grayson answered swiftly. "We would be glad to dine with you. I realize it is short notice, but I also think it would be fine if you wanted to remain with Avana as she trains for the rest of the day. That way, you can catch up with each other."

Avana, visibly brightened, exclaimed, "Thank you for your kindness, Uncle! I promise to make sure I finish everything."

The two friends left Grayson smiling after them as they headed back to the archery range. For the rest of the day, Killian followed Avana as she went through her exercises while chatting amiably. Later that night the three enjoyed a fine meal and discussed Killian's attempt to find the rescued man. At the end of the evening, Killian bid Grayson and Avana farewell. He promised to let them know as soon as he found Jare. Avana was sad to see him go, but now she felt truly hopeful of finding her father.

As Guard training progressed, Avana rose higher and higher in the ranks of the recruits. Not everyone liked her progress; Avana was a stranger, which made her ill trusted by the locals. But after a training exercise that nearly failed until she bailed them out, the other recruits looked at her more respectfully. Their task was to ride from the Thraicin River that emptied into Lonrach Lake, and back to the city without leaving any tracks or being recognized as soldiers. Her fellow recruits had little experience in concealment and were unimaginative in their attempts to carry out the exercise. Although already dressed in everyday apparel, they wanted to simply cover themselves and the horses in mud, and sweep away their tracks as they rode to the city.

Avana knew this was too obvious. Their horses were too fine to go unnoticed. She was right. A passerby readily pointed out a few of the recruits as soldiers, disqualifying them from the exercise. Instead, Avana suggested they allow the horses to be loose, as if headed for sale, in the tall springy grass around the lake until dark, and then head to the city. After the first failed attempt, Avana's idea was grudgingly accepted by some, but not all, of the recruits. About half of them decided to just ride in the lake water and make for the city. Again, they were eliminated from the exercise because they left muddy prints when they emerged from the water.

When darkness fell, at Avana's bidding, the remaining recruits rounded up the horses from the grass and rode them in the river and along the edge of the lake. When they reached the lake, they tied soft cloths to their horses' hooves, leaving hardly any impression in the dirt. Then they proceeded into the city.

Grayson was pleased to report that Avana's group was successful. He had hoped the recruits would listen to Avana, but he did not give her any special treatment. Grayson wished to be as fair as possible and not let on that he and Avana were related.

Very few people knew Grayson was her uncle. Nora knew because Avana felt it was rude not to tell her roommate why the captain sometimes visited her. Nora graciously kept the information to herself.

Avana was beginning to grow worried. Her three months of training were almost up, and there hadn't been any word from Killian since she saw him a month ago. She hoped he was just being very thorough in his investigation and that was why he was taking so long to send word. Finally, she was called to the office headquarters, where she was handed a note sent from Mahir:

Found Jare Sanger. He's willing to help. Your father is alive! Have lots to tell upon my return.

—Killian

Avana's heart leaped with joy as she clutched the note in her hand. Her father lived! Or, at least he had been when he helped

Jare escape. She raced to her room and told Nora her news. She danced around gleefully and then went in search of Grayson. He was as elated as she when he heard Avana's news. They were thrilled they now had real evidence!

A week later it was graduation day for the recruits. This was the day they would get their first assignment and have the right to be called soldiers of the Guard. Avana sat impatiently as she listened to all of the student accolades. Even when she was called to stand as her achievements were listed, she was unable to relax. Avana simply wanted to know her first mission. She desperately hoped it would allow her to meet with Killian in Amaroth when he returned. Her gaze wandered over the other recruits, each crisply turned out in red uniforms under their battle armor. The sun glimmered off the polished metal and Avana wondered who would be assigned in her group.

After what felt like an eternity of pomp, at long last, her name was called along with eight others. Her tightly knotted, worry-filled stomach relaxed a bit. Their assignment was to investigate a village called Amondale, along Lonrach Lake, that was suffering from goblin harassment and, if possible, eradicate the marauding creatures. Avana was content. This was a diffificult assignment, but it would keep her close to Amaroth. She was proud to be chosen for such a task. Each group was given a meeting room so they could begin studying the particulars of their respective mission. Avana purposefully walked to the room and quietly entered.

She was pleased to see Grayson already there, meaning he was the captain to whom they would report during the mission. She was surprised to find she was the only young woman in the group, given there were many female recruits. She was even more surprised when Grayson informed her that she was in command of the company. Avana sensed a slight air of disapproval from the men around her when they heard the announcement. This made her especially determined to prove she would not lead them astray. She must do well on this assignment.

Every night, goblins attacked the village to raid livestock herds living on the mountainside northeast of the village. Shepherds had disappeared with whole flocks; the ones who survived returned with terrible tales of fierce goblins making off with humans and animals alike, killing any being who tried to stop them. Amondale was only ten miles from Amaroth, but it was around the corner of the lake as a finger of the Cascades. It jutted out into Lonrach Lake, cutting off Amondale from a direct route to Amaroth. Avana studied the map lying on the table in front of the group. Already her mind was spinning with ideas of how to deal with the goblins. As she studied the map, she saw something that sparked her interest.

"What's this funny dot on the map?" she questioned the group.

"That's the Amondale Overlook. It's a rock formation that sticks up out of the mountainside and looks out over Amondale and Lonrach Lake," Grayson replied.

Hunched over the map and rechecking several other places, Avana confidently said, "That's where the goblins are coming from. A few years ago, I was traveling through the mountain edge and discovered they have a series of tunnels running along the base of the mountains. This overlook has all the hallmarks of a tunnel exit. They have an excellent hiding place and somewhere close by to plunder. There may even be a lair there, if they are taking as much as we have been told. My suggestion is that we blow up the lair and part of the tunnel. It won't be easy, but it will take care of the issue. The goblins won't come back to a place that has been discovered."

The entire group, including Grayson, stared at Avana for a

long minute. One of the men rubbed his sandy brown hair as he stared at the map.

"You may be right," he pronounced slowly. "I used to live in that area, and we would occasionally have a tangle with goblins. They would attack and disappear so quickly, we could never figure out where they were coming from. This makes much more sense now." He smiled at her a bit ruefully. "I'm Blane, by the way. I hope we can make this work."

The rest of the men murmured their assent. Grayson gave her an appraising look and said, "You're very likely right, Avana. That follows the pattern of most goblin attacks. They always want a way to escape. They rarely attack without a way to easily bring back their spoils. I will see what I can do about getting your team some explosives and related supplies.

Chapter 7

WITHIN TWO DAYS OF THEIR MEETING, the nine were fully equipped and ready to make the march to Amondale. After checking and rechecking their packs carefully, they each swung up onto a horse on the morning of the third day. Light filtered through the clouds as they rode out Amaroth's gate. The horses' hooves made a soft shuffling sound on the dirt road and kicked up small puffs of dust with each step. It was a little over a half-day's ride to Amondale over the mountainside or a day's march on foot. Although it was not a long distance, the mountain finger caused the road to wind back and forth making the journey much longer than it would have been otherwise. The group rode with the looming Cascade Mountains on their right and Lonrach Lake to their left. Steam rose off the lake as the rising sun heated the water. The group settled into an easy rhythm of riding as the sun warmed above them.

The trek over the mountain went smoothly and it was half past two when they rode into Amondale to the only inn, The Lazy Fish. The inn sat along the shoreline, offering a fine view of not only Lonrach Lake, but also the mountains. They ate a belated lunch in the main dining room and lost no time questioning the locals who were eager to tell their stories. Much of it was just hearsay from the tales the shepherds brought back, but one man had actually witnessed a goblin attack so they focused on questioning him. They also learned the names of some of the shepherds who had survived attacks. They split up, and with directions from the innkeeper, made their way to the home of each survivor.

Reconvening over dinner at the Lazy Fish much later that night, Blane told a story of a group of goblins that carried off more than a hundred sheep and killed five of the six men caring for them, with the sixth able to make an escape. One of the other soldiers, a tall lean man with dark features named Spear, shared a similar tale. Two young boys were sent up with food for the shepherds on the mountain. When they reached the pasture where a herd of cattle had grazed, they found a scene of carnage. Most of the cattle were gone, but those the goblins hadn't taken were brutally slaughtered, their bodies strewn over the ground. Three men were caring for the cows—two were found dead filled with goblin arrows, and the third was missing, presumed taken prisoner. Everyone else in the group had heard parallel stories to these.

Avana listened to everything with a sense of disgust filling her. It was nothing new to her, unfortunately. These were the same kinds of tales she followed when she lived in the Wilds. She asked each soldier if there was anything in common with the tales they had heard—time of day, or same place—anything they could think of. The group was quiet for a few minutes as everyone pondered the details, trying to find a connection.

Blane spoke first. "The moon. The strikes always happen on a moonless night. That's the common factor!"

"Excellent," Avana declared. "Goblins hate light, even if it's just the moon. Their raids have been very regular, almost two or three every month. The next one will happen on the coming dark night. Luckily for us, we've got a full moon for the next few days. If the goblins don't have a proper hole near the exit tunnel, we should easily sneak in and blow up the place."

"It probably won't be so easy," muttered a redheaded soldier called Tam. He looked gloomily at the others and sighed. He was the wet blanket of the group, but Avana knew his expert swordsmanship made up for it.

Avana nodded in agreement. "You're absolutely right, Tam. However, it's better to keep our plans simple and expect the unexpected than to try to plan for every possibility. Tomorrow let's ride up the mountain and scout the area. I want to thoroughly examine all raid sites and make a sweep of the Amondale Overlook. We'll need to be on our toes up there, but I'll wager there will be no goblins about. They have no reason to hang around except when the moon wanes and is gone."

Readying their horses the following morning, the company saddled an extra horse for their guide, Willum, to ride up the mountain. The shepherd agreed to show them the attack sites and take them to Amondale Overlook. Willum met them as they led the horses from the stables. He was a weathered man in his mid-forties, with wrinkled brown skin from years of exposure to sun and wind. He was one of the few men left in Amondale who was unafraid to go up the mountain. A single man, he desperately hated the goblins for taking his flocks and herds. His animals were his entire life, and he bitterly wanted revenge. He fought back against the goblins when they raided his sheep, but was severely wounded. Now almost fully recovered, he was more than happy to help the soldiers from Amaroth.

With Willum in the lead, the group carefully picked their way up the mountain. The ascent zigzagged through trees and over rocky outcrops until it reached the first plateau. Here, the mountain was covered with rolling green meadows, separated by windbreaks of trees, perfect for grazing. Willum led the group to each meadow where attacks occurred. Some still held the rotting animal carcasses, making the horses dance anxiously under their riders. Finally, the group covered all the raid sites, about a dozen in all. At each place, Avana dismounted and scoured the ground for signs of the goblins' departure. The trails were obvious, with grass badly trampled, until they reached the rocky ground beneath the towering pines separating the meadows. Avana knew she could follow the trail even over the rocks, but decided it would be faster to check the Overlook first, to confirm if her hunch was correct.

They stopped for a bite of food before heading to the Amondale Overlook. Willum was sure no goblins would be around in the daytime, as no one had ever spotted a goblin while the sun was up. Inwardly, Avana agreed with Willum's assumption, but still ordered the company to leave their horses and split into two groups, each taking a side of the Overlook to scout. If no goblins were spotted, then they would reassemble to comb the area for the exit.

Avana took one group and Willum the other. She pulled her cloak around her and signaled to the men to follow her. They crept carefully through the trees until they could see an opening ahead. Drawing near, they were impressed by what they saw. In the clearing, a mound of rocks stuck out of the ground, as if some giant happened to drop them there. One stone in particular towered above the others, extending through the trees and over the cliff's edge. It appeared to have a flat top, upon which one could climb and look out over Amondale and Lonrach. Avana smiled to herself. This was exactly the sort of place the goblins would choose for a tunnel exit—easy to protect, and easy to disappear into the maze of rocks around the base. Beside her, Tam caught her smiling at the rock formation and shook his head, muttering softly to himself about the chances of getting ambushed.

Avana's smile broadened. This place was perfect for an ambush—not just for the goblins, but also for them. Stealthily, they continued to scout the area until they were satisfied no goblins would attack them there. They met up with Willum's group, who had already found what they believed to be the tunnel entrance. Avana knew they made the discovery when she saw Blane grinning madly at her from beneath an overhang. It was nearly invisible from the front, as a twist of the rocks covered the hole from sight, making it look like a crack in the rock. Upon closer inspection, however, it was wide enough to take cattle through and stand three abreast.

Clearly, the goblins did not think they would be discovered, as the entrance was full of footprints. Broken fletchings from an arrow were scattered about with other debris. This was pleasing news to Avana, as it seemed to be a sure sign the goblins were unaware of the soldiers hunting them. It also made her a bit uncomfortable. This much carelessness could also mean a large number of goblins were close by and didn't feel threatened by an obvious doorway they believed they could easily defend. The soldiers and Willum pulled back from the rocks into the trees where they were hidden. Avana voiced her thoughts to the group and listened to the group's ideas. It was clear to everyone they had to explore the tunnel if they intended to demolish the exit.

Avana immediately volunteered herself. This would not be the first time she had gone into a goblin tunnel. Blane also spoke up, so it was decided the two should immediately begin exploration. Unsure how long it would take to explore the tunnel, they agreed if they did not return by first moonlight that evening, then the rest of the soldiers should assume something had happened to them. In her absence, Avana appointed as leader a soldier called Svengale, a blond haired, bearded giant from the Far North. Svengale was the eldest in the group, and had experience fighting raiders in the North before living in Amaroth. He was wily and able to improvise in tough situations. Avana trusted him to do what he thought best if the worst occurred.

Blane and Avana each took their cloaks, a small packet of food, along with their canteens. They also took a length of rope, and glow orbs—balls of tempered glass that, with a word spoken over them, would light up. When they reached the tunnel opening, Avana pulled out the rope and handed one end to Blane.

"It's best if we don't use any lights until we are sure there are no guards near the mouth of the tunnel. Loop this around your waist. That way we won't be separated in the dark," Avana whispered to Blane, tying the other end around her.

Blane nodded and did as Avana instructed. In silent accord, they stepped into the darkness of the tunnel. Staying close to the wall to feel her way along, Avana crept slowly forward. The tunnel began to gently slope downward and soon they lost the light from the entrance. Avana paused as she walked, causing Blane to stumble into her. She ignored his misstep and reached out with her senses to the tunnel around her. She felt the cool breeze coming from behind her from the entrance. Ahead of her, the air began to turn warm and stale. She listened to the soft echo of their breathing. The sounds carried directly back to them, meaning the tunnel continued for a distance. Satisfied they hadn't walked into a large area, Avana pulled her sword from its sheath.

"Stelenacht," she breathed over the blade. Immediately a gentle blue glow emanated from the blade, allowing her enough light to see in a small halo around her. Avana heard Blane's breath hiss when the sword began to glow, and she was surprised he kept his alarm to himself. Coming up next to her, he shook his head in wonderment. Blane knew there was only one sword with a blue glow. Again, he found himself impressed with the young woman beside him. The two continued on by the light of the sword. The tunnel twisted back and forth, but seemingly had no offshoots.

At long last, Avana saw something outside of the darkness that made her sheath her blade. Ahead of them was a faint glimmer of light. Stopping to pull their cloaks around themselves and their hoods up, Avana and Blane stole like shadows toward the ever-growing light. The air here was much hotter, and a foul odor floated faintly up to them. They could make out what looked like two large stones on either side of the wide opening of a cavern. With wordless stealth, they crept up behind the right hand stone and peered over into the space below.

Avana was struck with dismay by the sight before them. The cave was crawling with goblins. She counted more than fifty of the brutes as they lolled in obvious leisure around the cavern. This, at least, was a small comfort to Avana: surprise was on her and Blane's side. She noted the walls were full of ledges where one could potentially hide, thereby allowing them to traverse the cave without being spotted. The goblins were clearly not watching for intruders, and this would also be to the soldiers' advantage. Almost directly across from them, the tunnel continued into the mountainside. Avana knew this was how the goblins had come to this cavern. Something was missing though. She scanned the room again. There! A small hole in the wall, hardly bigger than the goblins themselves—this, Avana knew, was their escape route. Being cowardly creatures, goblins never tunneled without creating at least one escape outlet to the surface. Her adventures in other goblin holes had often been successful due to these escape routes. More than once they had saved her from capture.

Gently nudging Blane to get his attention, she pointedly looked back in the direction they came to communicate that she wished to return. Blane gave a short nod, and they carefully snuck back up the tunnel. Once Avana felt reasonably safe from the goblins, she spoke over Stelenacht again, so their return trek would be lit. When they reached the tunnel's opening, they slowly stepped out into the light, their eyes blinking rapidly trying to adjust. As they walked back to where the other soldiers hid, Avana could tell Blane was thinking hard about what they had discovered. She, too, was contemplating their find, but already a plan was forming, one she believed would work.

When they reached the rest of the group, they were met with questioning gazes.

"Well?" Willum asked impatiently.

Avana glanced at Blane who gave her a long look before he answered. "The tunnel is exactly what we thought. That's the good news. The bad news is, it leads to a cave holding fifty or more goblins."

With Blane's words, the soldiers' faces fell into grim expressions. Svengale broke the silence, voicing the thoughts of the group. "How are we going to destroy that many goblins, and their lair, with just nine of us? I mean ten," he amended after receiving a glare from Willum.

Avana sat down and leaned against a tree. "I have a plan," she said, "but it's going to be difficult. It will require our best effort. We sneak in and plant our powder charges, just like we planned to do. We just have to time the fuses right, so whoever lights them won't get blown up."

"But how will they escape?" Tam asked doubtfully.

"All goblin holes have an escape route that goes up to the surface. This cave was no exception," Avana explained. "You can get out through there and still explode the rest of the tunnel toward the Overlook. It's a two-man job inside—one person to light the explosives in the cave, and one to light the fuses for the tunnel. Everyone else needs to be hidden around the Overlook. With that many goblins some are bound to escape. The soldiers posted outside will pick them off with their bows. If we strategically place everyone, it will appear as if we have an entire, larger army surrounding the place."

The men again sat silently, digesting Avana's idea. Mattson, the youngest of the group, piped up, "I like it. Besides, I don't have any other ideas. When do we start?"

"I second that. It's a simple plan," agreed Jase, a tough-looking man who was previously a mercenary before joining the Guard.

The soldiers looked around at each other, nodding slowly in accord with Mattson and Jase. They deliberated a few more minutes but came to the conclusion this was the best proposition. They decided to head back down the mountain to make further plans and hash out the exact details. When they reached the inn, they quickly put their horses up for the night and met in the dining hall.

Avana laid out her plan again to the group, and they went through each part, creating a step-by-step strategy for the mission.

"Can you give me a ten-minute fuse?" she asked Mattson, their black powder expert.

"Yes, that shouldn't be too hard," he replied, scribbling down notes as they talked. Looking over at Svengale, Avana said seriously, "Could you spread out the men to create the aura of a larger army hiding in the woods?"

Svengale smiled wolfishly and replied, "With pleasure, lassie!"

They had not yet decided who would go back down the tunnel. Avana sighed to herself in resignation and volunteered for the job, saying that it only made sense, as she knew where the escape tunnel lay. Blane had been watching her, and when she spoke up he, too, said he would go back again. Avana gave Blane a grim nod from across the table, knowing their task would be the most dangerous. She was grateful to him for stepping up yet another time, and for keeping the secret of her sword. She wondered, though, if he would say anything to her about it later on.

After discussing the cave and tunnel dimensions, they decided they would need a dozen or so powder charges for the cave. These would be set in different places throughout the cavern, with three more as extras for the tunnel. Mattson determined he would need about two days to ready the explosives; he needed to ensure the timing was identical on all of the charges. This would also provide Svengale an ample opportunity to give the area surrounding Amondale Overlook a more comprehensive inspection. It was just as crucial for him to get his strategy right for the archers waiting above ground as it was for Avana and Blane to set off the explosives, especially if things went wrong for the two in the tunnel. Everything needed to be just right for them to succeed. *Ten against more than fifty were not exactly good odds*, Avana thought. Nonetheless, she also remembered the times when it was she alone against such a host, and she had come out alive.

CHAPTER 8

MID-MORNING, ON THE THIRD DAY after Mattson completed the powder charges, was the time they chose to attack the goblins. Avana was stern-faced as she looked over the group. There was a distinct possibility not all would survive this encounter. Avana did not fear death for herself, but the idea that some of the men under her leadership might die made her feel ill. She pushed her feelings aside, instead focusing on putting up a mental wall around her. This helped her on many occasions to survive the terrible things she witnessed. She thought only of the task at hand, carefully going over each step.

The soldiers reached the clearing where the Overlook stood. Then they wished one another luck, and took their positions. Avana and Blane quietly made their way to the tunnel, still taking every precaution against being spotted by goblins. Avana had decided simplicity was best when packing her gear. She only carried her sword, Saxe knives, the explosives, and a little food and water, wearing her dark cloak to cover it all. As she crept up to the mouth of the tunnel, she looked like no more than an errant shadow sliding silently along. Blane was to wait a half-hour at the mouth before going inside and setting his explosives in the tunnel. This would give Avana enough time to make her way down the tunnel and set the charges around the interior of the cave. Blane didn't like the idea of blowing up what he considered Avana's backup escape route, but he also trusted her, so he proceeded with the plan.

By the time she reached the tunnel, Avana was feeling the familiar rush of adrenaline that often accompanied her on her explorations. She was filled with a reckless glee, and threw Blane a cheeky smile, surprising him, as she turned to disappear down the tunnel. Now she was in her element! This time, going down the tunnel was a simple task. She was confident in her steps. She didn't even need the light of Stelenacht to make it to the end. Avana was at home in the blackness. She had to pace herself once she reached the cave. The light from the cavern quickly appeared ahead of her. At the first hint of light, any trace of hurriedness left Avana, and the recklessness filling her earlier was replaced with a steady, relentless drive.

Again she made her way to the rocks guarding the cavern entrance. Peeking over the edge she surveyed the room, looking for the best option to continue on. She decided to go to her left as a large outcrop would hide her from view and be a good starting point for her to place the explosives. The charges were set so that, once she planted the last one and activated it, the others would link together. Then they would go off in exactly ten minutes, which would give Avana just enough time to escape. Nearly invisible against the flickering shadows, Avana crept to the first ledge. She gently set the first charge and quickly moved on. She was able to easily make it around the room for the first eight charges, but to reach the lip of the next ledge she would have to cross an opening.

The goblins were working busily in the cave, preparing for their next raid on the village. The raucous sound of their laughter grated against Avana's nerves, and the pounding of smiths' hammers on dark metal blades rang in an evil song. For the moment, too many goblins stood nearby for her to sneak through. Avana waited patiently, knowing eventually they would have to move. Luck was on her side, for unexpectedly, a fight broke out among the goblins across the cavern from her. This brought the group closest to her snarling and running to join the melee. This was all Avana needed, and she slipped across the opening with wraithlike stealth. She continued setting charges as she drew near the small escape tunnel. Finally, she held only one. This she intended to put in the mouth of the tunnel, to prevent any goblins from following her. As she reached the lip of the last ledge before the tunnel, she saw something that made her stop in her tracks.

A crude cage a few feet from her held a man. Clearly this was one of the shepherds who had been captured. He was bloodied and bruised, but seemed very much alive as he huddled in the back of his enclosure. No goblins guarded him, for they had all run off to join the fight at the end of the cave. Avana knew she couldn't leave him, but she also wasn't sure she could open the door to his cell without any tools. After a moment of indecision, she purposefully crept over to the cage. Avana softly called out to the man as she stole up to him, "Don't cry out! I'm going to free you. We must leave quickly."

The man started at her voice and turned fearful eyes toward the black shadow that spoke to him. Kind blue eyes met his as he crawled toward the cage door. Avana studied the lock—a large rusty affair she might be able to open with one of her Saxe knives. Pulling out a knife, she deftly worked the lock. For a moment, it seemed like it wouldn't budge. Then, with a raspy, grating noise, the lock sprang open. Carefully opening the door, she beckoned to the man who gazed at her with shock and curiosity. He pulled himself out and crouched painfully next to her.

"Come, into the tunnel," Avana said pointing to the goblins' escape tunnel.

Abruptly a shout went up from the goblins. They had been spotted! Hurriedly, Avana pulled the last charge from her pocket and set it. Now the other explosives were activated and it was a race against time. Pushing the man into the tunnel, she quickly clambered after him. It didn't take long for the goblins to reach the tunnel and follow them.

"Run!" hissed Avana, "Don't stop, no matter what!" Soon the tunnel behind them was full of goblins. Avana pulled out her knives as they ran through the tunnel heading for the surface. She wouldn't have room to maneuver with her sword in these close quarters. The injured shepherd could not outpace the goblins, and they quickly overtook them. Avana cut down the first goblin as it rushed at them, and slashed at another as it came up behind. She continued to back her way out the tunnel, trying desperately to escape. The goblins tried to overwhelm their opponent, with several coming upon her at once. Hacking and cutting wildly, Avana felt this might be her last stand. All of a sudden, the ground beneath them rocked wildly and the tunnel vibrated with a terrible roar. The charges had finally gone off. The goblins fell down in a panic, and even Avana was sent stumbling. Pulling herself together, she grabbed the shepherd by the arm and practically dragged him up the tunnel. "Move!" she yelled over the rolling noise of the still collapsing rock.

With a last desperate burst of energy, the man flew into a broken run, with Avana at his side. After a sharp turn, Avana could see daylight up ahead. This brought fresh life to their legs and they came bursting out of the tunnel. Disoriented for a moment by the light, the two staggered into the forest. Once Avana's sight had adjusted, she realized they were on the farthest side of Amondale Overlook. She continued to run deeper into the forest with the shepherd. A goblin arrow hissed by her head and thwacked into the tree beside her. They were still too exposed, and began to duck and dodge through the woods as more arrows rained down around them. Some goblins made it out of the tunnel and were in hot pursuit. *Where were the rest of her soldiers?*

A moment later a volley of arrows from the trees ahead came whining down upon the goblins. Now it was their turn to run for cover. Avana pinpointed the place where her men hid, and pulling the shepherd along, kept low under the brush until they were upon the soldiers. They found Svengale and Griff launching another round as they came about the bushes hiding them.

"Well done, missy," Svengale commented as he drew his bow again. "We've got the blighters on the run now."

Only a few goblins now remained and they were backtracking toward the rock face, seeking protection from the soldiers and the sun. Seeing their retreat, Svengale turned to Griff and ordered, "Get Tam, Lander, and Spear, and clear off the rest of those goblins. Better go quick before they have a chance to escape."

Griff nodded as he slung his bow over his back and pulled out his sword. He loped off through the woods toward the other soldiers. Avana watched the Overlook, carefully marking the spot where the goblins were hiding. They didn't stand a chance against the soldiers coming after them. Her concentration was broken when she heard a cry of pain from the shepherd who had been sitting behind her. In their flight to safety, she had forgotten he was injured. Mentally berating herself, Avana swung round to see Svengale already offering the man a drink of water. After a long swallow, he managed to rasp out, "Thank you. You saved my life. I didn't think I would ever make it out of that terrible pit."

Avana smiled. "You're welcome. I couldn't just leave you behind. I'm glad you were able to make it out with me."

"Nearly did me in," the man said dryly. "Forgive me for not mentioning it sooner, but my name is Aric. I was down there for two weeks and nearly gave up hope."

"No need to apologize, Aric, I'm Avana," she said with a small laugh. "Introductions weren't on the top of my list back there either."

Svengale laughed heartily at their exchange and added, "Just be grateful she got you out! This girl is a tricky individual. She's not one to let something go once she has it in her head."

Loud yells from the rocks and garbled curses from the goblins distracted them from their conversation. Metal clanged loudly in the clearing and the sounds of a scuffle ensued. As suddenly as it had started, the clashing ended and then they heard only silence. Spear appeared, followed by Griff, Tam, and Lander. They were furiously grinning, their armor splattered with blood. The foursome walked over to the group hidden in the brush. As they did so, Mattson, Jase, and Blane also appeared, followed by Willum, who looked happier than they had ever seen him. When Willum saw Aric he rushed to his side.

"You're alive, my friend!" Willum said ecstatically.

"Just barely," Aric replied, smiling at Willum. "Those brutes nearly got the best of me, but this young lady here managed to get me out."

By now the rest of the group had reached them, and there was celebration all around.

"We did it!" Blane practically crowed. Tam stood next to him, shaking his head in amazement. "It worked," he said, "it actually worked!"

"Of course it worked," Svengale glowered at him. "Avana knew what she was doing. She's got the fire of her father in her."

Avana looked up sharply when she heard this, and saw the puzzled looks of the men around her. She stared hard at Svengale who simply rolled his eyes and sighed in exasperation, "They need to know who you are, lassie, if they are going to serve with you."

Still eyeing Svengale, Avana slowly spoke. "My father is Caleb, son of Aramis. I carry his sword, Stelenacht."

A mix of shock and amazement crossed the faces looking back at her. Blane looked satisfied though. Now he understood the mystery of her sword.

"How did you know who I was, Svengale?" Avana hedged suspiciously.

Svengale gave her a teasing wink and answered, "Your uncle Grayson told me. He didn't want you getting into trouble without a friend."

Now some of the jaws around them dropped. "Your uncle is Captain Grayson?" Spear asked, a bit dazed. "No wonder you're such a good soldier and strategize so well. Your family is famous for those qualities."

The rest of the men murmured their assent to this. "Yes, he's my uncle," Avana said matter-of-factly. "But I don't want to be treated any differently for who my family is. I'm not anyone special."

Tam spoke this time. "Well, I, for one, owe you an apology. I didn't think you could pull this whole thing off. I wish I had known who you were sooner. I would have trusted you more. But the fact stands, you plotted the destruction of an entire goblin host, and their hole, and managed to accomplish it. On top of that, you rescued this fellow! After this experience, Avana, I would follow your lead even if you wanted to attack a dragon's den."

"I second," Spear piped up.

"And me!" Griff announced, and the concurrence of this sentiment went round the group ending with Svengale. "Looks like you have some dedicated soldiers," he told Avana, smiling kindly at her.

Avana's heart swelled with gratitude and pride as she looked at the men standing around her. She wished her father and Killian were here to witness the moment. Blushing brightly, she waved away their accolades, causing teasing laughter to rise up from them. To avoid further embarrassment, she ordered that they go back to their horses hidden several hundred yards away.

After the adrenaline rush from the fight, Avana felt drained as they rode back down the mountain. She also felt a huge sense of relief. Her first assignment—not only had she survived, but she had succeeded! This was far more than Avana hoped for considering the odds. She also knew her anonymity was gone. She had been revealed as Caleb's daughter, and a feat like the one she and her soldiers just accomplished would soon be known across the whole land of Arda. She wondered what would come of this. For the moment she simply wanted to return to Amaroth and hear Killian's news of her father.

That night the soldiers celebrated with the people of Amondale over the goblins' demise. The villagers were grateful beyond measure to be freed from the terror of the evil creatures, and thanked the soldiers over and over again. A feast was held and many toasts were made to the safety and health of the heroes. Avana cared little for the spotlight and soon slipped away from the festivities. She made her way back to the inn and fell exhausted into bed.

The town was quiet the next morning after the revelries of the previous night. The soldiers said their goodbyes only to Willum as they swung onto their horses and began the journey back to Amaroth. When they arrived and rode through the city gates, the hustle and bustle of city life quieted them. No one knew of their triumph, and the group was happy to keep it that way. It was worth it to give Amaroth peace and safety. Winding through the city, they made their way back to the Guard barracks.

After seeing to their horses, the group notified Commander Ruskin and Captain Grayson of their return. They convened in Grayson's office to give their report. Although Avana tried to minimize her part in the story, the rest of the men were quick to sing her praises. Ruskin and Grayson were surprised to hear about the number of goblins, but were pleased to hear how efficiently the soldiers took care of them. After everyone had reported, Ruskin and Grayson found they had no questions. However, they agreed some words of praise were in order.

Ruskin was quite happy with the whole affair. He and Grayson had deliberated over who should be in Avana's assignment group and clearly they had chosen well.

"Good work, soldiers," Commander Ruskin smiled. "You went up against some ugly odds, but were resourceful enough to succeed. I couldn't have done any better myself! What do you think, Grayson?"

Grayson beamed proudly at Ruskin. "I'd say they did a fine job, especially under the circumstances. But that's part of being a soldier in the Guard." Turning serious and looking at Avana and the men he said, "You never know exactly what you will get out there. You must be prepared for anything, and be ready to do whatever it takes. Obviously you figured that out."

The soldiers nodded in agreement to this as they thought back to the surprise of the goblins. Blane spoke up then, "Commander Ruskin, we have a request."

"Yes?" Ruskin said curiously.

"I know it is customary to go out on several assignments with different soldiers until you find a group you fit well with, but we talked it over—we want to stay together. And Avana doesn't know this, but we want her to continue to lead our group," Blane said earnestly.

Avana's eyebrows shot up at this declaration, and her shocked look caused Grayson to give a snort of laughter. Ruskin was also a bit taken aback, but he was satisfied his previous perceptions of Avana as a leader were correct.

"I will grant your request, Soldier Blane, on one condition: that Avana is promoted to captain. Is that satisfactory, Blane? And, Avana, are you in accordance with this?" Ruskin asked with a smile toward Avana.

"Absolutely," Blane declared.

Avana felt completely baffled. She, a captain? After her first assignment? This was incredible. She couldn't believe it and for a moment considered saying no, but decided that would be ridiculous. Instead she slowly nodded her head as she started to wrap her mind around what just happened. Commander Ruskin promoted her, and she had a loyal team behind her. Now nothing could stop her from finding her father!

With Avana's acquiescence to the promotion, Ruskin declared the debriefing over and declared they should all have a week's leave before their next assignment. This announcement was a great boon to the soldiers who were still tired from their mission. As they left to go to their respective rooms, Grayson caught up to Avana and stopped her.

"Killian is in Amaroth, Avana." he spoke quickly. "I know you are tired, but I'm guessing you would rather see him and hear his news than rest?"

"Yes, if that's all right," Avana replied enthusiastically. Her body was weary, but rest could wait. "Where is he, Uncle?"

"The Highwater Inn. He's staying for several days. You have my permission to visit him, not that I would be able to keep you here. I'll meet you in five minutes by the fire pit."

When they reached the Inn, they found Killian sitting in the common area. Avana was happy to see Killian, but she could scarcely wait to hear what he had to say about her father.

Settling back into his chair after greeting Avana and Grayson, Killian began, "Jare Sanger was not an easy man to find. His time as a prisoner had made him extremely wary and suspicious. Took me an entire day before I could get him to talk to me. But once I convinced him I was there to help look for Caleb, he was willing to work with me. He really had a lot of useful information. The best part is, he seemed very certain your father is still alive. Jare told me the great goblin chieftain, Garzvahl, wants to keep your father alive. Why that is, neither he nor Caleb knew. He also told me, and showed me on a map as best he could, the locations of the different goblin holes they'd been in. The bad news is, he doesn't know exactly where they were going next when he escaped . . . but he is willing to show us the general area."

Hope filled Avana's heart. This was incredible news! She wished Jare knew the place where the goblins kept her father, but at least she had places to start looking.

"Thank you, Killian. I can't believe you were able to find out so much," Avana squeaked.

Grayson was also pleased with Killian's findings. "Where do we start, then?" he asked.

Killian pulled a map of Arda out of his pocket. "I believe we should start here," he said as he unrolled the map and pointed to a small village. "This is where Jare Sanger was rescued by Captain Marco and his soldiers. If Caleb is still being held in the same place they were being moved to during the escape, then it should be close to this village. As you can see, the village is near several different rocky outcrops. Any of these could be a hiding place for the goblins."

"Well, then, we shall search them all," Avana declared.

"Yes, that's what we'll have to do," Grayson said, looking determined. "It won't be an easy task though. It's a vast area with many places to hide a goblin hole."

Killian gazed at both of them gravely. "He may not even be there anymore, but it's a good place to start. If you don't mind, I would like to help you continue searching for Caleb. I must confess, being a merchant really is not the most exciting job. Hunting for a long lost Ranger is far more interesting. However, if you believe you now have the investigation under control and no longer need my help, I will understand."

"Stop helping? You have been a bigger help than I could imagine. I'd be a fool to deny your request," Avana said firmly. "We *need* you, Killian."

"You really have been invaluable," Grayson added. "It gives me peace knowing you will be part of the quest for my old friend."

The dwarf looked gratefully at the two sitting before him. "I am honored to be of service," he said simply.

For the rest of the evening, they continued to study the map and plan possible ways to effectively search for Caleb and the goblins. When Avana returned to the barracks for the night and lay down, she found she couldn't sleep. Her mind was spinning from the events of the last few days. She knew now that some of her fears were relieved. Ever since her father's capture, she was frightened he had been killed like the rest of her family. Now, she knew he really was alive! This was the best thing she could have hoped for. It was going to be difficult to track him down, but with the help of Killian and Grayson, she could do it!

Chapter 9

AVANA AND GRAYSON TOOK KILLIAN'S NEWS to Commander Ruskin, who was pleased with the turn of events. The part of the Wilds Jare had pointed out was largely uncharted territory. Though there were goblin nests known to exist in the area, their exact locations had not been pinpointed. Ruskin charged Avana and her men with the task of thoroughly mapping out the area. He wished to know the precise locations of every goblin hole. It would be beneficial for Amaroth to have a working knowledge of goblin whereabouts. This, in turn, would allow Avana to search for her father.

The Western Seas were a long journey, but often Amaroth sent soldiers to protect the villages along the shores. Because it was such a distance and difficult task for novice soldiers, Ruskin decided to send Captain Grayson with the group. Grayson was older and wiser, and he had the ability and knowledge to make contact with the Rangers—something Ruskin knew would prove invaluable in searching out the goblins.

After receiving their next mission, Avana and her men spent their week off relaxing and recovering from their first assignment. When the week was up, they reconvened to begin preparing for Ruskin's task. Because of the length of the journey, they would require extra provisions. Grayson took charge of this as he had the most experience. They chose steady horses with good stamina for the trip.

Finally, they were ready, and started down the road into the Wilds. Their expedition would take them across the Wilds, through the middle of Greenwood Forest, and then into the rocky barren Wasteland between the Forest and the Western Sea. The road continued all the way to the main seaport of Tir Falken. However, the group did not intend to go all the way to the city. Their search would take them through the rock country south of Tir Falken.

The beginning days of travel were the hardest, as they settled into a rhythm of riding all day, and camping at night. Though they were all good riders, there were still sore muscles at the end of the first day when they stopped to rest. Avana didn't complain, however. Riding was a significant improvement over walking. She had crossed hundreds of miles on foot before, and she was grateful for the horses that carried them.

Crossing the Wilds without incident lent speed to their journey. They made it halfway and now they would have to go through the Greenwood Forest. Though the Forest was thought to be mostly safe for travelers, there were some parts that worried Avana. Growing up and living on the edge of the Forest, she knew the dangers of what lay deeper within. The outer borders of the Forest were quite habitable and held few surprises, but the trees started to change as one approached the heart of Greenwood Forest.

Here, the atmosphere became very close and damp. The trees grew to massive, towering heights with moss hanging from them. Eventually it turned into a proper rainforest. Vines dangled in endless mazes from the heights of the trees. Brilliant emerald butterflies flitted to enormous magenta hanging flowers covering the tree trunks. White and azure blooms carpeted the ground, while ruby red hummingbirds hovered and darted among the petals. The center of Greenwood Forest was also home to the rare purple spruce, whose needles could be ground into the deadliest of poisons; yet its roots, when properly dried, could cure any malady.

The forest dripped constantly in a quiet melody. Such strange creatures dwelt there. The elusive and gentle two-headed zeeback was highly prized for its chocolate-striped coat, but if tamed, it made the fastest steed in all of Arda. The predatory orange-and-black thylacine wolf-cats with spine-ridged backs roamed here. These aggressive and merciless killers hunted in packs, using a relay system of runners to chase their prey to exhaustion. Avana remembered well the warnings of her parents not to wander into the depths of the forest. She had no wish to lead the company into a pack of thylacines or other dangerous creatures.

Riding back into the forest brought countless memories to Avana, though they were not particularly near her old home. The cool shade of the trees reminded her of the times she and her family picnicked together under the great boughs. She was hit with an overwhelming sense of loneliness as she rode along. To have those times of peace and safety back was something Avana wished for deeply. She hoped eventually her future would lead her to a new place of such love and a real home.

Chapter 10

AVANA'S FAMILY HAD LIVED in the northern part of the Forest. The road they now took was many miles to the south. Though she hadn't spent significant time here, Avana still had some knowledge of this road. She and Grayson took the dangers of the Greenwood seriously. They rode with their weapons ready at all times and slept with them close at hand. One of the biggest transformations the company noticed, as the Forest changed, was the bioluminescence of the night. Flowers gave off a pale glow in various colors, and the moss hanging from the trees lit up in fluorescent greens. Even the incessantly peeping frogs left a trail of bright yellow slime.

They were now traveling through the heart of the Forest. All day peculiar eyes had watched their progress and the group felt the awful tension. Their horses were uneasy, and Avana knew it must be something truly alarming to frighten these proud steeds. She worried they were being stalked by a pack of thylacines. That evening they set a double watch as they settled down for a tense night. Avana fell into a troubled sleep. The presence of some creature or being was causing unrest in the Forest, and her body perceived a foe nearby.

In the midst of the darkest part of the night, something woke Avana. What she had detected she wasn't sure, but it brought her instantly to a state of extreme wariness. She saw Spear and

Mattson awake on watch duty. They did not seem bothered. Abruptly, a shrill whinny of terror came from the horses tethered close by. Leaping to her feet, Avana searched the semi darkness around them for any unwelcome creatures. Spear and Mattson also scrutinized the surroundings. Then Avana felt it: a subtle rumbling. This is what had awakened her.

But what was it? Avana wracked her brain. From the depths of the glowing forest she heard a gruff snuffling, the sound causing the hairs on the back of her neck to prickle. Again she felt the ground vibrate against the soles of her boots. The horses were now in full panic and pulled mightily against their ropes. Avana quickly awakened the rest of the company. As she did so she thought she saw a large dark shape streaked with green moving through the forest. Now fully alarmed, she drew her sword.

Suddenly they heard a loud grunting snort, and the ground beneath them shook again. The horses uttered scream-like whinnies and broke their ties, taking off into the Forest before anyone could stop them. Something was coming toward them rapidly. All at once, dozens of black forms came charging through the woods.

"Wild boars! Climb if you value your life! We can't outrun them!" Grayson warned.

It was too late. The gigantic hogs were already surrounding them. Snarling and slashing out with their tusks, they thundered around the soldiers. They were nearly man height and black as night but for their glowing red eyes, and vivid streaks of green slime crisscrossing their backs. The group was distraught to find their blades did little to pierce the boars' tough hides. Only Stelenacht seemed able to do significant damage. Avana fought desperately against the terrifying creatures that seemed mad for flesh and pressed persistently at the company.

Avana made a frantic hack at one of the boars, slicing it from snout to tail. The smell of their companion's blood created pandemonium among the hogs. They turned on their own, and began to rip into the unfortunate beast. Seizing the opportunity, the soldiers raced to the nearest trees and clambered up as fast as they could. In an unlucky moment, Spear tripped and fell at the base of a tree trunk. Svengale and Lander were above him in the boughs. They cried out in distress as they watched one of the monstrous pigs turn and slice Spear's leg open as he tried to pull himself up. The soldiers heard a high-pitched whine then a solid thwack as an arrow buried itself deep into the back of the offending boar.

An enraged squeal erupted from the boar and it lunged away from Spear. Blane drew back again and sent another arrow thudding into it. The pig shook itself in pain and anger, trying to rid itself of the shafts. This action was enough to allow Svengale and Lander to pull Spear into the tree with them. Again smelling the fresh blood, the rest of the hogs turned toward their next quarry. Huffing with deep grunts, the injured swine took off into the Forest with most of the group following it. The remaining boars harried the body of the first boar until it was torn completely to shreds.

The soldiers in the trees looked on in horrified disgust at the beasts' behavior. The hogs lingered long at the site, harassing and fighting with one another over the remains. Finally, when the first rays of sunlight began to filter through the trees, they left uttering low grumbling growls. Avana's group exhausted, they huddled in the trees for the better part of the night. Spear's leg had been cut to the bone in a wound running from his knee to his ankle. He lost a great deal of blood, and was delirious and faint with pain.

Once they felt sure the wild boars were gone, they descended from the boughs. Lander and Svengale carefully lowered Spear down. Grayson grimly inspected the wound and thoroughly cleaned it. He looked over at the purple spruce at the edge of the clearing and thought, *the root of that tree would have come in handy. If only it wasn't so difficult to dry properly for use.* He worried about the length of time Spear had gone without his injury being treated. Boar tusks often carried toxic bacteria that would cause a wound to fester and the flesh decay. Grayson knew that, without their horses, they would be hard pressed to reach their destination. Thankfully they still had their provisions, cached up in the trees to keep inquisitive animals out of the packs, and thus were spared from the marauding hogs.

Talking it over with the rest of the company, it was decided they would continue on through the Greenwood and send out a signal for the Rangers when they came out the other side. The Rangers would have the proper medicine for Spear's leg. Grayson feared that if the Rangers could not be reached, and if Spear sickened, they probably would not make it to Tir Falken in time to save him.

Futilely they searched for their horses, and were disheartened when they saw tracks leading farther into the woods. Wearily they continued on through the Forest on foot. Every night Grayson cleaned Spear's injury and re-bandaged it. Their going was slow, but they had passed through the rainforest section and were now drawing close to Greenwood's edge. Two weeks after the attack, Spear's wound was not healing properly. He was having headaches and his leg throbbed incessantly. He toiled on in silent agony, as the poison became a raging infection that wracked his body.

Avana was extremely grateful to see the end of the forest. The Wasteland on the other side of the Greenwood was covered in knee-high green grass growing in sandy earth. Rocks of all sizes dotted the countryside, making the ground uneven and difficult to traverse. This area was used solely for grazing purposes and few people roamed it. Grayson led the company across the rough terrain in a southwest direction, heading toward an old ruined tower set on a hill amid a large rock formation.

Around the whole of Arda, there were many of these old towers now in crumbling disarray. Long ago they were watchtowers to communicate between the kingdoms of men, dwarves, and elves. Now the Rangers used them to signal one another, and people seeking out the Rangers also used them. Grayson told Avana and the rest of the men about the system the Rangers used. Each site was supplied with a large quantity of firewood. To seek audience with a Ranger, all one had to do was light a fire on the top of the tower and keep it burning until a Ranger answered the call.

Spear was now extremely sick. He no longer could put weight on his leg and had become so weak they were forced to carry him on a makeshift stretcher. Grayson pushed the company to their limit as he hurried to reach the tower. They were all relieved when the hill came into view. They struggled up to the summit with their burden, careful to not jostle Spear more than necessary. Grayson and Blane quickly set to work lighting a fire with the wood on hand. Now they would just have to wait.

CHAPTER 11

AN ENTIRE DAY PASSED before they saw a lone figure riding across the stone-filled plain toward them. The person was clearly a Ranger, judging by the dark weather stained cloak and the shaggy horse he rode. A cowl obscured the man's face, but his gray beard was visible. Avana realized with delight that she recognized the stranger.

"Grandfather!" she called out from the hilltop.

Throwing back his hood the man lifted clear blue eyes and answered, "Hello, Avana, you are well?"

"Yes, I am well," Avana smiled down at him. "But one of my companions is very ill. He was ravaged by a wild boar. We need medicine now. He won't make it to Tir Falken."

The Ranger nodded and ascended the hill. Grayson was relieved to see Aramis, head of the Rangers. They quickly introduced him to their company as Aramis rifled through his saddlebags to see what he had with him. He settled on a tea and poultice. Aramis methodically brewed the tea, while Grayson applied the poultice to Spear's leg. The wound was an angry red and pus drained freely out of it. Spear writhed in agony as Grayson smeared herbs over the gash.

While Aramis prepared the tea, the rest of the soldiers analyzed the fabled Ranger before them. Though his hair was gray, he still seemed hale in mind and body. He questioned them closely on their adventure so far. He looked at them contemplatively when they spoke of the loss of their horses, but kept silent, motioning them to continue their story. When their words came to a close, he spoke thoughtfully. "So, my son may still be alive. I am heartened by your tidings. They are better than anything I could have expected."

The tea ready, he turned from Avana and the soldiers and brought Spear a steaming cup. Speaking in a low tone, he raised the tea to Spear's lips, carefully helping Spear until the cup was emptied. Avana noticed the tea had a calming and numbing effect. Already Spear was less agitated, and the lines of pain that creased his face had relaxed. The company felt their own tensions diminish at Spear's relief. Soon, Spear was soundly asleep, unfettered by his aching leg.

The rest of the group too settled down to rest. Aramis joined them, and he gave insight on the territory they were planning to explore. He decided to spend the night with them to make sure Spear was healing properly. Avana was grateful for the time her grandfather devoted to them. In some ways he was the stranger he'd always been, yet he managed to be the loving grandfather she remembered. She was dejected when he finally left the next day. Though she had little contact with Aramis since her family's fracture, she still felt a strong tie to him.

They stayed on the hilltop for another week while they waited for Spear to regain strength. Between the poultice and the tea Aramis left, Spear improved quickly. The fever left him and the poultice drew out the redness and infection. Eventually Spear felt well enough to walk, though he was slow and weak. At Spear's insistence the company again started on their way toward the barren lands behind the small town of Mahir. Every day Spear grew stronger and the wound healed faster. Soon it had closed up and only a bright pink line remained.

Now the soldiers could focus on the task at hand. Taking the information Aramis gave them, they began searching for the goblin holes. The first one they found was little more than a surface tunnel that led to an empty cavern. It had quite obviously been unused for a significant period of time. Regardless, they diligently marked the location on the map they were creating.

The second cave they discovered was inhabited by goblins. But judging by their low numbers and how small the cavern was, the soldiers did not think Caleb had been held there. This cave too was marked on the map. The third goblin nest they came upon was considerably larger, and Avana's hopes skyrocketed when they uncovered a heavily used tunnel.

Again, Avana and Blane found themselves together as they searched the third hole. She and Blane soundlessly crept down into the tunnel. Avana's heart raced as they made their way. What if her father was below them at this very moment?

The tunnel opened up around them, and ahead, light began to filter toward the duo. Harsh voices could be heard as they approached the cavern. This was no small cave. Rather, it was a great fissure in the ground. Ghosting up behind a large rock, Blane and Avana looked over the expanse before them. An entire goblin city stretched out across the space. Avana felt sick to her stomach. It would be incredibly difficult to reach the slave pits she knew were somewhere below her, and they had to get closer in order to search properly. Sitting back against the stone, she looked at Blane. Avana did not wish Blane to join her as she went down among the goblins, but she knew he would not let her go alone.

After a whispered conference they headed back up the tunnel to inform the others. Grayson and Svengale were not surprised by their findings. None of the company was happy when Avana and Blane told them their plans. Blane had the idea that while he and Avana were searching for Caleb in this particular cavern, the rest of the group should continue scouting and mapping of the land. Both parties would meet back at the Ranger watchtower when they finished. Grayson was particularly disturbed by this plan. He did not like leaving them without backup. Nonetheless, he saw the wisdom in this strategy and eventually acquiesced.

Avana and Blane took their packs and headed back down the tunnel. It would take several days to completely scout out the city and then a few more to reach the tower. They again hid behind the large rock as they plotted their course. The ramshackle goblin city was not set in any pattern. Buildings teetered precariously off rock ledges and sprawled across the floor without a set road or path between. At first glance, Avana couldn't see any of the deep pits the goblins favored for holding prisoners. But, after a second time going over the area closely, she discovered a grated over hole not far from their location. Blane too had spotted a prison about halfway across the city.

Now they had somewhere to start. Both of them knew it would be tricky to make it unseen through the colony, but Avana had done so before and Blane trusted her ability to keep them hidden. The city had several hundred goblins living in it, and dozens of tunnels coming to and from it. Because they lived underground, the goblins did not have a set time for sleep, but certain hours of the day were less heavily trafficked than others when the creatures would rest.

Avana and Blane decided to check the pit nearest their location. There was a great deal of rubble surrounding it, making it less dangerous for them to observe as the debris provided cover. Also in their favor was the fact that since there were so many goblins around, the slave pits were left mostly unguarded. The goblins were very cocky, sure that no prisoner could escape without being seen. After a solid hour of slipping behind rocks they made it to their destination.

Unfortunately, the hole was empty. Though disappointed, Avana was not surprised. Goblin slaves generally did not have a long life expectancy. That was one of the reasons why Avana had been so glad to hear that her father was still alive. The goblins were cruel taskmasters and often killed prisoners just for making a mistake or angering them. Avana hoped they would have better luck at the next pit.

Yet they did make one useful discovery. Along the wall of the cave, near the prison pit, was another smaller, shallower hole in the rock. The place was hidden from unfriendly eyes by large boulders and some unused buildings. It was little more than a hollowed spot of the earth, but it had no goblin footprints in the dust inside, making it the perfect place for them to rest and hide out. Here they relaxed for a bit and left their packs before continuing on.

CHAPTER 12

THE COMPANY DECIDED they should circumnavigate the city to check for more pits along the outer perimeter. It took them the rest of the day to do so. They found two other holes, but neither held prisoners. They retired to rest back at their hiding place. After several hours of sleep, they awoke again and strategized their approach to the inner city prison.

The goblins' *nighttime* was when the group deemed it best to attempt their move. It would be a while longer before this, so they again rested as they waited. When the appointed time came, they began to carefully move into the city where the buildings grew sturdier and more plentiful. Slowly they continued, keeping to the shadows, and slipping from building to building, spying on many of the goblins' activities as they went.

Avana and Blane passed by something greatly alarming. A smithy with a gigantic forge had been set up with dozens of huge weapons inside in various stages of creation. They wondered what sort of creatures could wield these arms, but neither could decide what they had been built for. At last they came upon the large slave hole they were looking for, guarded by three large goblins. Avana was elated, sure this was an indicator the goblins held an important prisoner.

Together, Avana and Blane climbed up onto a rooftop over-looking the prison. They crouched on the far side of the roof peak and peered over. Below them they could see the pit covered in a heavy metal grate. They could make out the form of a lone figure at the bottom. Avana's heart galloped wildly in her chest; what if this was her father? The goblins patrolled the perimeter of the pit. No other goblins were in the area, but as they were in such a populated part of the city, it would be nearly impossible to access it without discovery.

Avana and Blane conferred in whispers. Neither of them felt right leaving the prisoner without a rescue attempt. But how could they get him out without alarming the entire city? After a heated discussion they settled on the idea of distraction. They would set fire to the forge they discovered, and its buildings. This would hopefully cause enough confusion and chaos to allow them a suitable amount of time to escape.

It was a dangerous plan, but not only would it provide them time to rescue the prisoner, it would also ruin the weapons they had stumbled upon. They each took on a task. Blane would rescue the prisoner and Avana would set the fire. After their decisions had been made, Avana scaled down the roof and headed back to the smithy. Blane was to wait until he saw the first flames licking up the building before he should strike.

Avana reached the shop and pulled out her striker and flint. Taking a piece of cloth she used to polish her sword, she tore off a bit and lit it. This she placed on a beam of the structure. Tearing off other strips, she did the same thing to the buildings around her. Already the forge shop was burning. Flames crawled up the side of the dry boards, quickly turning into an unstoppable inferno.

Blane watched carefully from the rooftop. He smelled the smoke and saw the flames at nearly the same time as the goblin guards. Taking his bow he brought down the first guard. Howls of dismay arose from the other two at the sight of their dead comrade. In rapid succession Blane put an arrow in the chests of the other guards as they frantically searched for their attacker.

With a cursory check of his surroundings, Blane scurried down to the pit's edge. Searching the guards' bodies, he located the keys to open the prison door. Rapidly he unlocked the door, and heaved it open with a grinding thud. The prisoner below him rose and wearily climbed out with Blane's help.

He stood a head taller than Blane with cat-like gray eyes, golden hair, and pointed ears. Blane was a bit dissatisfied the prisoner was an elf and not Avana's father, but he was glad to liberate anyone from the goblins. The elf's dirty, threadbare, black and gray clothing hung from his emaciated frame. His face pale and haggard, his prominent cheekbones stuck out sharply.

Blane and the elf hurried off together when harsh bells began to clang loudly as the fire was discovered. Soon the area around the smithy was swarming with goblins, but the conflagration Avana had created was burning at a mad pace, consuming every-thing around it. The goblins' buildings of dry timber combusted, the fire growing with hunger each moment. A panic rose among the goblins as dozens rushed to the scene. Frantically they hauled buckets of water to try to extinguish the inferno.

Blane used the chaos to escape back to the hiding place he and Avana discovered. It was touch and go as they spent precious minutes dodging crazed goblins, but the fire made the creatures oblivious to everything else. Sputtering a bit from the smoke billowing from the blaze, Blane and the elf retired to the alcove. Now they would just have to wait for Avana.

"What's your name?" Blane asked.

The elf seemed to consider this question before answering, "I am Nedanael. It's been many months since I have spoken to another creature besides those vile goblins. Thank you for rescuing me. I gather you are not alone?"

Blane smiled, "You are most welcome. And no, I am not alone. My fellow soldier Avana set the fire that served as our distraction. I expect her to be along presently. My name is Blane."

The elf nodded tiredly, and closed his eyes as he relaxed back against the rock. Blane offered him food and water, which Nedanael gratefully accepted. Though the elf was clearly starving, Blane was impressed by his ability to hold back from gobbling down the food. Instead he wisely nibbled away at it so he would not be sick. Time began to stretch on as they waited for Avana. A niggle of worry ate at Blane's mind. It was nearly two hours since they reached the hiding place. Avana should have been there by now.

Perhaps she was delayed, he reasoned. Besides, with the goblins still in an uproar, it was unwise for him to venture forth to search for her. Two more hours dragged by. Now Blane was sure something was wrong. Avana was in trouble. Beside him, Nedanael sensed his unease.

"Your companion has not returned," he commented, as Blane grew restless.

"Something has happened to her," Blane replied curtly. "I must search for her."

"I will come with you. Perhaps I can be of some assistance." Nedanael asserted.

Blane gave him a concerned look, "You are weak. Avana is not your responsibility. It would be well for you to escape while you can."

Nedanael snorted, "I am not as frail as I look! The smithy your friend burned was where I worked. Among my people I am a skilled weapons maker. The goblins took great pains to capture me. They needed me to create the arms you must have seen. I don't know what creature was to wield them, but they must be impressive. I fear what it means. They tortured me cruelly to bend me to their will. I would never freely work for them," he added in a vengeful tone.

"It was your work then! I understand now. We wondered about the craftsmanship. It seemed too well made for a goblin. I am sorry for what you endured," Blane finished, looking on the elf with respect.

Nedanael again bowed his head in acknowledgement then spoke, "Let us not waste time. Your companion is undoubtedly in danger."

Blane agreed, and the two stole back into the city. They were drawn to the loud noises of shouting and commotion. They approached stealthily and Blane was aghast when he saw Avana bound tightly and surrounded by dozens of goblins. They seemed to be arguing over what to do with her. He noticed Stelenacht lay on the ground on the outskirts of the mob. The goblins gave the sword a wide berth and jabbered angrily at it. With heated voices they gesticulated madly between Avana and the sword, making it clear they were afraid of both her and the blade.

Though the goblins' fear was in their favor, Blane was unsure how to use it to their advantage. Blane knew Stelenacht would not repel him, but it would not respond to him the way it did Avana. Turning to Nedanael, Blane noticed the elf's eyes glittered with the light of an unspoken proposal.

But all he said was, "I can free her. Cover for me with your bow."

Before Blane could protest, Nedanael was gone. Blane was frustrated with the enigmatic elf, but readied his bow to do as he was asked. He watched as Nedanael furtively crept forward. Belatedly he realized Nedanael didn't even have a weapon! What cryptic plan did the elf have?

Nedanael was hidden within a burned out building only a few feet from Stelenacht, when he turned his head to Blane and gave a subtle nod. Blane took this as his signal to shoot when Nedanael broke cover. Springing to action, the elf leapt into the midst of the goblins and snatched up Stelenacht. Blane sent an arrow into the nearest goblin, adding further confusion to the pandemonium. Lifting the sword high above his head, Nedanael called out in a commanding voice, "Stelenacht!"

The sword blazed to life brighter than Blane had ever seen it, and the flash temporarily blinded and paralyzed the goblins around Nedanael and Avana. With swift strides the elf was next to Avana grasping her sword. He hewed down the guards holding her and cut her bonds. Around them the goblins stirred from their paralysis. Again the blade in Nedanael's hand pulsed its blue flame, sending the goblins into writhing paroxysms. Taking her by the hand, he raced back to Blane and the three hurried through the city to the hideout.

Avana was bloodied and bruised. A gash on her temple sent blood dripping down her face and covering a purple welt on her left cheek. The worst was a stab wound to her thigh that produced a limp she could not conceal. Regardless of her injuries she insisted they depart from the goblin hole immediately. Taking up the packs, they crept back to the tunnel.

Upon reaching the outside entrance, they were dismayed to find it was nighttime. They would have to continue their flight if they wished to escape the goblins, for it would not be long until their route was discovered. Doggedly they resumed their getaway. They jogged onwards with a steady pace until dawn, steadily drawing away from the goblin hole. When the sun came up in earnest, they found shelter beneath an overhanging rock and collapsed, wholly spent. It was many minutes before any of them felt the energy to speak.

Finally, Blane broke the silence. "Let me wrap your leg, Avana, to stop the bleeding."

Wearily Avana nodded and she began to tell her tale of capture as Blane attended her injury. "The fire trapped me. It spread so quickly from the buildings that I was hemmed in by it. It was only after a building collapsed that I was able to get out. Unfortunately, by then the goblins were everywhere. I was shaky from the smoke and didn't have the strength to fight. They caught be and tied me up. They couldn't handle Stelenacht though. It burned them when they touched it. This angered them and they beat me, but did nothing else because they were so preoccupied with the fire. The goblins were trying to decide what to do with me when you swooped in and rescued me. Thank you, Elf. I'm sorry I do not even yet know your name."

"I am called Nedanael. I am pleased to make your acquaintance," the elf responded.

She introduced herself and then with quizzical expression, continued, "How did you wield my sword like that? And more importantly, how did you know its name?"

Nedanael gazed at her, "Because I forged it for Caleb. I assume you must be his daughter, for a blade like Stelenacht will only respond to its maker, its owner, or a descendant. I am a master smith . . ." And he expanded on what he had previously told Blane. Avana took in this information with great interest. She sorrowed for what the elf had gone through, and her thoughts went out to her father. Though disappointed they had not found her father, Avana rejoiced over freeing Nedanael.

The three rested for a number of hours under the rock's protection. But all too soon they set out again. It was necessary to put many miles between them and the goblin hole before darkness came. Again, several days passed until they reached the watchtower. They found it empty, and settled down to repose and wait for the remainder of their company to arrive. While they waited, Avana pressed Nedanael for information about her father.

She learned her father was very young when Nedanael made the sword for him. He was close to her age, the elf reckoned. Avana felt let down when Nedanael revealed he had not seen Caleb since then. However, when she explained that Caleb had been held in the same area as Nedanael, the elf grew excited. There was another important prisoner in the city at one point during his captivity. They never met, but Nedanael reasoned there was a good chance it was her father. This lifted Avana's spirits a bit after the letdown of not finding Caleb. She would always keep up hope of finding him.

Another two days went by before Grayson, Svengale, and the rest of their group arrived. It was a merry meeting as they found themselves together again. They recounted their tale of searching three more lairs, but none of them held any prisoners. When the time came for Avana and Blane to tell their story the rest of the company was captivated by the account. Grayson congratulated them and praised their efforts. It was a hard task they had completed.

After all the stories were told, they decided they should rest another day then head back to Amaroth. Nedanael agreed to travel with them at least partway through the Greenwood. Then he would make his own journey back to his elf kingdom. Though they were still on foot, they made a much shorter trip to the Forest compared to their previous journey.

Nedanael listened to the story of their previous passage with interest. When he learned of the loss of their horses he announced, "If they were lost in the Forest the elves would have found them and brought them back to the elven land. I will try to return your horses to you."

When they reached the edge of the Greenwood, Nedanael left them with the intent of bringing them their horses when the company came out on the other side. All were grateful when their crossing of the Greenwood was without incident. The luminescent heart of the forest was still as strange and ethereal as before, but no creature disturbed their travel. Upon arriving on the verge of the Wilds, they delayed their journey and awaited Nedanael.

Their stay was short as Nedanael arrived early the next evening, bringing their lost horses with him. As he had predicted, the horses had been found by the elves and given sanctuary in the elven kingdom. They were unhurt and looked healthier than before their stay. The company was delighted Nedanael had returned their animals, and thanked him profusely. He only smiled and replied that bringing back their horses was a small token compared to the freedom they had given him. Nedanael would not stay the night despite their insistence, and bidding them farewell, he returned to his own people.

With the return of their horses, the soldiers were able to hasten home. Relief spread over the group as they rode into sight of the walls of Amaroth after their lengthy journey. It felt good to be home. On their arrival they made a short report to Commander Ruskin, giving him the map they created. Ruskin was again pleased with the courage and thoroughness of the group, despite their many difficulties.

CHAPTER 13

OVER THE NEXT THREE YEARS, Avana grew in fame for her successes in the Guard. She almost always completed her missions, and she never lost a soldier. This made her widely popular to the people of Amaroth and to the Guard. She matured in skill and wisdom. She was matchless in sword fighting and could devise a plan for any situation she encountered. Avana found she was happy in the Guard—she was busy and often in danger, but more importantly, she had friends. Grayson Hale became like a father to her while Blane, Svengale, and the rest of the men were her trusted allies in any mission or situation. Avana and Grayson kept in contact with Killian as the trio searched for Caleb. They systematically continued to examine any possible leads about where Caleb was being held. Sometimes only one of them could check an area, while other times all three would join in. Through it all, Avana and Killian continued to write to one another, keeping updated on each other's adventures. Avana often felt like her search for her father was foolish, but she could not let go of her hope.

Something was happening though. As they continued to search for Caleb, more and more goblin disturbances began to occur. Attacks started on Halfor's kingdom and it had come to the point where Killian was needed at home almost constantly. He hadn't seen Avana in more than a year and missed her. No one, not even the Guard of Amaroth, was sure why the sudden spikes in attacks were occurring. All they knew was things were getting progressively worse. Then something terrible occurred. Halfor's son Halever was captured by the goblins. The dwarf kingdom was torn deeply by this blow. However, the news was kept quiet to the rest of the world in an effort to aid the group assembled to rescue him. Halfor sent a secret message to the Guard of Amaroth asking for their help. Killian was placed in charge of the dwarves tasked to find Halever. The Guard quickly pledged their help to Halfor's cause and promised him their best men. With a heavy heart, Killian set out for Amaroth with fifty dwarves.

When Avana was called into Commander Ruskin's office and heard the news of Halever's abduction, she was shocked and felt heartbroken for Halfor. She could sympathize with Halfor's pain from her own experiences. She eagerly agreed when Ruskin asked her to partner with Killian to search for Halever. She missed her old friend, and was looking forward to seeing him after their long separation. Ruskin assigned her one hundred men to work with Killian's group. However, when Ruskin told Avana where Halever had been taken, it brought back painful memories. Halever was presumed held in the Wilds, close to her old home. Commander Ruskin hoped, since she knew the area better than anyone else, that this would give the search and rescue party a greater chance for success. Already Avana was going over in her mind the places where Halever could be. There were a limited number of goblin holes, which improved the odds of their search. Unfortunately, a few of them would be very difficult places to conduct a rescue due to their location.

Two days later Killian and the dwarves marched into the city of Amaroth, making their way first to the Guard barracks. Killian saw Avana from a distance as he walked through the

Guard. He was immediately struck by the changes in her. She was no longer the girl he remembered—Avana had matured into a woman. She wore a sleeveless dark green tunic covered by a fitted leather vest and brown breeches. Muscled arms held a sword as she practiced a drill. Any trace of awkwardness had left her, and her movements were quick and sure. Her chestnut hair was pulled back skillfully so that it was practical as well as fashionable. In short, she was beautiful, and Killian suddenly felt tongue-tied in her presence.

As she turned around to block an imaginary blow, she saw Killian standing across the courtyard. Instantly, her face lit up, and Avana sheathed her sword. Killian was startled when she ran to him and embraced him warmly.

"My old friend, you have returned!" Avana greeted him merrily. "It has been far too long since we were last together. I sorely wish we were coming together under different circumstances though. I am terribly sorry to hear about Halever. We will search every goblin hole the length of the Wilds to rescue him if we have to."

Killian relaxed at her warmth, realizing she was still the same person she'd always been. "I too wish the circumstances were different. I am so glad to see you're well, Avana. News has spread of your triumphs all the way to the dwarf kingdom."

"Ah, it's mostly luck! And my soldiers are excellent. It's hard to fail when you have good people to rely on," Avana said dismissively. Killian noticed, however, she didn't deny his words, and she had an air of confidence that wasn't there before.

"So I assume you already have a bit of a plan in mind?"

Avana nodded with a satisfied grin. "Indeed I do. It involves lots of sneaking in dark places, which may be a problem with how many men we have. But if we do come up against a goblin host, I'd rather have a few soldiers to help us out."

"Well, then, lead the way." Killian enthused, "You know the area better than anyone."

"Yes, I'm afraid I do," Avana replied slowly. A shadow crossed her face as she remembered her old home. "Sometimes I miss those days, Killian—to have my family back, to hear my mother's voice calling me inside for the night. It was all so long ago! I would love to have a place to really call home. The Guard has been a perfect fit for me, but eventually I want to settle down. Then the only adventures I'll have will be the ones I make for myself. It's tough always being on the move." She gazed seriously at Killian, a bit surprised with herself at her frank admission.

Killian reflected on her words before answering. "I think you will find that someday, Avana." Inwardly, he realized he cared very much for her, and hoped her dream would come true.

"I hope you're right," Avana said sighing. Then putting aside her worries, she declared, "Come, we have much to prepare and plan."

Together they walked deeper into the labyrinthine ways of the Guard. It took four days after Killian's arrival to outfit the company with needed supplies and to make satisfactory plans. On the fifth day, they set out. It would be at least a two-week march before they reached their destination. During this time Avana's friendship with Killian was renewed and the two were nearly inseparable. Killian was impressed with the loyalty of the soldiers Avana commanded. They would do anything for her, as she was like a queen to them. Her core group—Blane, Svengale, Spear, Jase, Tam, Griff, Mattson, and Lander—were all fiercely protective of her. They were her right-hand men, to whom she delegated most tasks.

Avana speculated for a long time about where they should camp. It would not be easy to shelter one hundred fifty soldiers and stay undetected. Eventually, she decided on a small valley positioned in a central location from the goblin holes they intended to search. The valley had a stream running through it that would provide them fresh water, alongside green grass for their pack animals to graze. On one side, it had a cliff face that turned into steep overhangs where they could take shelter if the weather turned. The other side of the valley was ringed with a dense shrub brush that, from a distance, made the valley invisible. When they reached the valley, Avana was pleased to find no signs indicating it was recently used. To the best of her knowledge, few people knew of its existence, but occasionally, a wandering shepherd would occupy it.

When they reached the valley and pitched camp for the night, Killian found the dale to be perfect for their necessities. He was fascinated by Avana's ability to remember so much about an area she hadn't been to for years. Her attention to detail and to their needs was carefully thought out. Her heritage of wise kings and fearless Rangers truly showed through.

They decided to scout out the nearest goblin hole the following day, to get a lay of the land, even though Avana felt it was the least likely of the locations to hold Halever. When she had wandered the Wilds, this hole had rarely held any goblins, but she and Killian both believed it was imperative to check even the least likely of places. They agreed only twenty soldiers were needed—fifteen men and five dwarves. The spot was at least two hours from their position, if Avana remembered correctly, so they would need to leave at dawn to give them as much daylight as possible to search the goblin hole.

Gray mist wreathed the valley as they rose the next day. Lander, Svengale, and Tam joined the other twelve soldiers Avana selected to go with her and Killian. The five dwarves fell into line with them and strode purposefully over the wet grass. It took them two hours, as Avana had expected, to reach the hole. Avana struggled a bit when it came time to find the entrance, but eventually she pinpointed the location. The group cautiously made their way to the goblin den, taking care to keep hidden as much as possible. They warily entered the low cavern serving as the entrance. Avana led the way, with the rest of the group coming down a few at a time in case they were attacked.

When they reached the inner part of the cave, Avana was surprised to see it no longer looked as she remembered it. Even worse, it appeared to have been recently used by a great number of goblins. This disturbed her, but she decided they must press on. Finally, the entire company was inside the cave. Avana ordered the soldiers to spread out and thoroughly search the cavern for anything that could offer more information about the goblins or Halever.

She called Killian over to her. "Something doesn't seem right here," she confided in a low voice as she looked around the grotto.

"I agree," Killian whispered. "All the signs suggest the goblins are here, but where are they?"

Where are the goblins indeed! Avana wondered. Abruptly, she realized what had bothered her about the hole. There was no escape tunnel, nor even a connecting passage to another goblin cave. Her eyes again roved the cavern to make sure she was correct. As she beheld the cave, she noticed a large smooth slab of stone at the back of the cave. Two dwarves and four men had just walked out onto it while she looked their way.

Horror filled Avana. "Get back!" she yelled to them in a fear-filled voice.

Killian's gaze flew to the soldiers Avana yelled at, his eyes widening in surprise and fear. "It's a doorstep stone!" Killian shouted. "Get off it. It's a trap!"

But, as he spoke, the stone cracked in half, as if touched by magic, sending dwarves and men tumbling into the abyss below.

"No!" Avana cried in a strangled voice, its sound lost in the chorus of hoarse yells and curses emanating from the hole in the floor. Immediately, goblins began swarming up from the opening. Their ugly gray hides were covered in rude battle armor, clearly showing they had been waiting for an attack.

"Fall back!" Killian yelled over the terrible din. The remaining soldiers frantically ran back toward the cave entrance. They knotted together against the overwhelming force coming toward them. Fiercely they fought as they headed for the mouth of the cave. Goblins scurried overhead like giant spiders dropping down in front of them, blocking their path. Killian fought them off, slaying one after another as they slowly pushed forward. Avana held up the rear, fighting like a mad woman. Stelenacht blazed bright blue, reflecting her adrenaline, and momentarily caused the goblins to drop back. "Go!" she roared, as the soldiers made a final bid for the cave entrance. Upon reaching it, they broke into the sunlight, doggedly staying together.

A stream of goblins followed after them, cringing under the bright sun. The soldiers continued their desperate retreat. Not one of them had escaped injury in the devastating fight, and it hampered their speed. Avana was dismayed to see Lander had a terrible laceration running across his back and down his side. She was amazed he was alive after sustaining such an injury. Avana's mind raced as she tried to remember a place where they could hide. It came to her that a shrub forest was nearby, and she began leading them to its safe refuge. The farther they came from their hole, and the longer they were in the sun, the weaker the goblins became. Sunlight sapped their strength, whereas darkness enhanced it. Taking advantage of this, the soldiers fired volleys of arrows at the goblins chasing them. This further discouraged their pursuers. Soon the soldiers were able to disappear into the shrub forest, and the goblins gave up their pursuit.

The soldiers hid, drawing further into the scrub trees, before eventually coming to a halt. Avana was grim. They had lost six from their group, and the rest were in poor shape. She was seriously worried about Lander. He had the worst wound, and she could tell it was taking a toll on him. Suddenly, he collapsed into the dwarf in front of him, causing the rest of the men to come flying to his aid. Quickly they made a stretcher out of branches from the scrub trees around them and laid Lander upon it. What few medical supplies they had were used to staunch the wound as best they could. They also took time to patch up the injuries of the rest of the group. Once this was done, they agreed the best action was to make directly for camp. The sooner Lander made it to the camp's doctor, the better.

Avana had sustained only minor cuts herself, and she helped to support one of the men who received a deep cut to his calf muscle. She led them back to camp, but their slow pace took them nearly all day. When they finally limped back into the valley, they were met with shock and dismay over their condition.

Avana silently made sure the injured soldiers received the best care possible, personally seeing to it that Lander was given first priority. Then she stiffly walked to her tent and closed the flap. She threw herself onto the low cot and sobbed into her pillow. Guilt wracked her heart. She had failed her men and Killian. How could she have possibly missed the signs of the trap? Doorstep stones were a classic goblin trick. They fooled the unwary into thinking it was just a regular rock until it gave way beneath them. Soldiers died because of her mistake and she didn't know how she could live with herself.

Killian was tired and sore that evening. He was also worried about Avana. She was stonily silent on their return to camp and spoke only the minimum to the doctor. Her absence at supper only caused his worry to grow. He sat brooding by the fire when Svengale approached him, looking deeply concerned.

"Killian, I need your help. Avana has holed up in her tent ever since your party returned. She won't eat, won't come out, and I can barely get her to speak to me. You're the only one here she will listen to. Please, try to reason with her and find out what's wrong."

"I'll see what I can do," Killian said anxiously. He hurried to Avana's tent where the sound of crying from within stopped him cold. In all the time he had known her, Avana never cried, not even when she was recalling her family. Killian's heart broke for her, and he desperately wished he could rush in and comfort her. He knew it would only anger and embarrass her, so instead, he composed himself and called out, "Come to dinner with me Avana, the stew is delicious. You need it after the day we've had."

"No, thank you," was the distinct reply. Killian wavered a moment, wondering what he should do next. He decided to risk her wrath and boldly opened her tent and strode in. He knelt beside Avana and placed a hand on her back.

"Leave me, Killian," came Avana's muffled voice from the pillow.

"No," he replied firmly. "You are coming with me to eat. No arguing." To his surprise and relief, Avana slowly got up. Then rubbing the tears from her eyes, she stormed out to the fire with Killian close behind her.

The fireside was empty, as everyone else had already eaten. No one noticed as Avana wordlessly ladled stew into her bowl. Killian also helped himself, and settled down next to her as she leaned against a log. At first Avana picked at the stew, but after a few bites, attacked it with the ravenous hunger Killian knew she had been carrying from the stresses of the day. He ate his meal in silence, waiting for her to break her reserve. When her bowl was empty, Avana set it aside and stared coldly into the fire. At long last she drew her knees up to her chin and spoke without taking her eyes from the fire. "I failed, Killian," she said roughly. "I should have seen the trap, but I didn't. I was too cocky and self-confident that I knew what I was doing. I was a fool! I don't deserve to be called captain. My men trusted me, and today good soldiers died because of me . . ." With these last words she choked into sobs and buried her face in her arms.

It's time to take a chance, Killian decided. Without replying, he simply put his arms around Avana and pulled her into him. She didn't resist. Instead she leaned into him, sobbing quietly on his chest. Speaking softly, he said, "Every good leader makes mistakes. In war, sometimes it costs lives. But the men who died today knew this was a possibility going into it. They were trained for these situations, and could have just as easily spotted the stone."

"But it's my job to see things like that beforehand!" Avana protested into his shirt. "I'm done with the Guard. My three years are up anyway. They don't need a captain who makes mistakes."

Angered by this statement, Killian replied, "You are not a quitter, Avana. Your men need you." And after a moment he added, "*I* need you, Avana . . . I'm falling in love with you."

Killian felt Avana still in his arms at his admission. Pulling back for an instant, she seemed to look at him with new eyes. She remembered all the adventures they enjoyed together, and her hand went to her neck, brushing the necklace he bought for her.

"Are you really?" she asked, her eyes questioning.

"Yes," he replied with certainty.

Without hesitating, Killian dared to do what he had wanted to do for quite some time—he kissed Avana. She was shocked, and for a second she was frozen. Then she found herself kissing him back. His lips pressed against hers with warm electricity that thrilled her. He buried his hand in her hair and gently pulled her closer. Avana melted into his embrace, wishing the moment would never end. They kissed with all the heart two fighters could give and, when it was over, they both drew back with shy smiles.

"I'm sorry," Avana said huskily. "For everything. I'm a bit dense sometimes. You should have said something sooner. I've cared for you for a long time, but I wouldn't let myself see it."

"I'm not entirely sure I knew exactly how I felt either. It was better this way, I think," Killian said mildly. "You needed time to grow without me."

Avana looked at Killian with deep affection. "I believe you're right, Killian, but I missed you terribly when we were apart. You were the first friend I made after my time in the Wilds."

"How could I not befriend you? When I first saw you, fighting off those goblins alone, I was impressed by your bravery. You needed our help, but you were intelligent, wily, strong, and dreadfully beautiful," Killian laughed tenderly. "You had me enthralled simply by your intrigue, and the more I got to know you, the clearer it became that I was falling in love with you."

"And you persisted even when I was traveling far, far away," Avana marveled.

Killian grinned wickedly at her, "Dwarves don't give up easily! I hoped that someday you would come to love me, but I wasn't going to push you."

"You're a perfect scoundrel, Killian," Avana declared as she nuzzled into his neck. He smelled of wood smoke and leather. It was irresistible and comforting at the same time, so she closed her eyes and relaxed as she leaned into him.

Killian's heart felt like it would burst as he held Avana in his arms. He didn't care if the rest of camp saw them embracing. Most knew that he was very close to her. Svengale had even teased him about it on more than one occasion.

After a while, Avana yawned. Kissing her lightly, Killian

said, "You need to get some sleep, Avana. Tomorrow is a new day and we must regroup and plan before the goblins discover us—though, I do wish we had more time to mourn the loss of our friends today."

Avana sighed. "Indeed we must, and I agree it doesn't seem right to move on so quickly after lives have been lost. I feel strongly that the goblins in this area still have Halever nearby, especially after seeing the large force that attacked us. They wouldn't have so many goblins gathered unless something important was going on. Now the element of surprise is lost to us. How are we going to find exactly where they are holding him?"

"I'm sure we will catch a break and figure out a way," Killian said confidently. Then he helped Avana to her feet and walked her back to her tent. With the pleasant taste of a goodnight kiss still on his lips, Killian found his way back to his own tent and fell instantly asleep.

In the wee hours of the morning, before the sun had even thought about shining, they caught the break that they needed. Guards had been set to keep watch over the camp and one of them had captured a goblin scout. In exchange for its life, the cowardly creature was happy to inform them where Halever was being held. However, it cackled evilly as it told them with cruel words that there were more than four hundred goblins assembled to guard the prince. The goblin spitefully mocked their puny rescue attempt, denouncing their ability to defeat the goblin hordes.

When Avana heard this news, she was both crushed and elated. Now that they knew where Halever was, they could make a bid to rescue him. But they were going to need help to get him back. As she retired back to her tent to try to get some sleep, Avana's eyes were drawn to the giant wolf skin she used as a blanket. Her mind flew back to her years in the Wilds. Perhaps it was time to seek help from some old friends.

Chapter 14

THE NEXT DAY SHE ASKED KILLIAN, Svengale, Blane, and Spear to ride with her. She didn't tell them where they were going. Instead she made the utmost haste to the edge of the Greenwood Forest where the Wilds lands met the trees. They rode among the trees until they came upon an overgrown clearing in the forest. The long charred remains of a house could still be made out from the undergrowth. Killian realized Avana had brought them to her old home. Stopping in front of the house, Avana turned to them, "Please trust me in what I am about to do. *Do not* draw your weapons, no matter what happens! It is imperative that you do as I say."

Dismounting from her horse, she gestured for the rest of the group to do likewise. Leaving their horses in the clearing, they followed Avana through the trees. They walked a short distance into another opening in the woods, much larger than the first, covered by low grass. This was where Caleb had grown his crops. They came to the edge of the grass and stopped. Avana pulled a small silver horn from her pack. It was intricately carved with all kinds of animals and was inlaid with ivory. Killian had never seen it before and was intrigued. Putting it to her lips, Avana blew a long high blast. It rang brightly in the stillness of the forest and seemed to fill the clearing.

For a moment there was silence. Everyone held their breath

and waited to hear an answer. From a great distance away, a chilling howl broke the stillness. It undulated up and down, starting deep and powerful then ending on a high lofty note. *What was that?* Killian thought, as the men beside him looked around nervously. Suddenly, he spotted something through the trees. A large creature spirited through the forest toward them.

It broke through the trees and stepped out into the clearing across from them. It was a gigantic wolf, as big as a draft horse. Its shimmery white coat reflected the sun, giving the creature a fiery glow. The wolf's eyes were bright gold and they studied the group with keen intelligence. Nothing could have prepared the men for this, and they stepped back in fear. Only Svengale seemed unperturbed.

Avana removed her sword and Saxe knives in a gesture of respect, then strode forward and said, "Hail, Finris, High Chieftain of the Wild Wolves of the North."

The massive wolf growled a response in the common tongue, further shocking the men, "Hail, Avana, adopted daughter. You know the penalty for calling upon the Wild Wolves of the North without cause. Why have you dared call on me?"

"We seek your aid in rescuing Halever, son of Halfor, king of the dwarves, High One," Avana replied while bowing her head.

Surprise flickered through his eyes at her words, and he answered her. "This is indeed a worthy cause. You have what help we can give. Come near, for I have missed you!"

Forgetting all propriety, Avana raced across the clearing and threw her arms around the white wolf. She buried her face in his thick fur, ran her fingers through his silky pelt. Killian looked on incredulously as she hugged the great beast. This was beyond anything he'd ever seen.

Suddenly, another wolf appeared beside Finris. "Fallon!" Avana cried joyfully and turned to him.

"Sister!" the wolf yelped in reply. In a flash, they were wrestling together, the wolf growling and snapping with such ferocity that Killian and the men feared for Avana's life. Abruptly, they broke apart, both panting in gleeful delight. Avana made a low gravelly noise that sounded like rocks rumbling together, and Fallon answered her in kind. Killian realized they must be speaking the language of the wolves. Avana also seemed to address Finris who growled back in turn. Killian was utterly bewildered. This was the stuff of legends, and yet here he was, witnessing what was only told in bedtime stories. He was greatly puzzled by Svengale's lack of surprise by the whole situation. This would require a great deal of explanation.

Finally, Avana and the two wolves, Finris and Fallon, approached the group. Killian realized Finris was the older of the two by a great deal. Streaks of gray mingled with the silver hair around Finris' face and over his back. He also was slightly larger than Fallon, and carried himself like a king.

"I'm sorry for my secrecy and any confusion I caused you," Avana told the group. "Long ago, the great kings could communicate with almost all creatures. They formed a friendship and alliance with the Wild Wolves of the North. In times of old, they fought side by side against common enemies. However, it was always out of the mutual respect of one king for another. When the kingdom fell and the Rangers were formed, the Wild Wolves gifted them with this horn," she gestured to the silver horn hanging at her side, "as a way to honor their agreement. The caveat was that it was only to be used at times of greatest need, under pain of death, to prevent the Rangers from ever trying to enslave the Wolves. My father gave it to me as his eldest child and heir."

Spear responded, voicing the thoughts of the group, "So this is how you survived for so long in the Wilds on your own . . .

except you weren't alone, were you? You were with them," he finished gesturing toward the Wild Wolves.

"Yes, that is exactly right, Spear," Avana smiled with the look of conspirator. "Svengale, you don't look surprised in the least! How did you guess my secret?"

"Between your wolf pelt and the gaps in your story, I pieced together the truth," Svengale said. "Not everything from legend and fairy tales is false. In the North we still believe in Wild Wolves and Ice Trolls, as every once in a great while, someone from my lands encounters one."

"Thank you for not spoiling my surprise," Avana laughed. "Come now, I am forgetting my manners. Introductions are needed. It is my honor to introduce you to High Chieftain Finris, and his son, Fallon. Wolves of the North, these are my trusted friends, Svengale, Blane, Spear, and Killian."

"Well met, brave warriors," Finris rumbled and Fallon nodded in turn. "Now tell us how we may help."

"Let us sit, and I will explain," Avana replied. The wolves lay down and Avana leaned up against Fallon as she began to explain the details of what happened. She missed nothing, and took full responsibility for the mishap the day before. When Avana told them four hundred goblins guarded Halever, Fallon growled softly and Finris shook his great head with a sigh.

When Avana finished her account, Finris rested his head upon his enormous paws and let out a long low whine. "Something is not right in all of this. I have lived almost two hundred years, and only once before have I seen goblins massing like this—before the Great War. I fear for what this means! Nonetheless, we will help you, daughter. I believe I can assemble fifty pack members from the area. They, along with your force, should be enough to destroy the goblins or, at least, rescue Halever." Finris continued thoughtfully. "We must act quickly though.

Every moment we hesitate, the goblins will grow stronger. You have a plan, I presume?"

"Yes, at least an idea," Avana replied. "I believe we launch a full scale attack to draw them away and then send a few in to rescue Halever. I don't think the goblins will expect us to confront them openly."

Finris brought his head level to Avana's and said, "That is a bold plan indeed. But I think under the circumstances it is the best option. Let us waste no more time." Standing up again, Finris commanded Fallon, "Alert the packs of what is to be done. Meet us on the edge of the valley so you do not frighten their animals."

Fallon stood up and answered, "As you wish, Father. Good-bye, Avana. May we soon meet again!" Then he sprang away with a terrible howl.

Finris turned back to the group and spoke, "Let us return to your camp and prepare. It may take your men some time to get used to the idea of fighting with my kind. Avana, ride upon my back, as you used to. I have missed you, and it would please me greatly."

Avana gestured to Killian standing next to her, "Only if Killian can come, and if the rest of you don't mind leading our horses back," she added, glancing toward the other men.

"Go ahead, Avana," Blane smiled. "It won't be a problem."

"The dwarf can come," stated Finris deliberately. Then he shook his entire body and stretched, yawning as he did so and showing off a red tongue and sharp, gleaming teeth. Finris lay down again beside Avana and she climbed up onto his back. Killian followed her, wondering if he really wanted this seemingly dubious honor. Svengale, Blane, and Spear headed back for the horses as Finris advanced into the forest. Killian clutched Avana, full of nerves. Riding a horse was bad enough, but a wolf was worse! Avana sat completely at ease astride the wolf and Killian envied her ability to do so.

Finris vibrated from beneath them, "Quit squeezing my sides, dwarf. I'm no wayward horse. I will not let you fall. Perhaps I should, though, as you are obviously in love with my Avana."

Killian felt his face go red, and he tried to relax his grip. He began to stammer something out when he realized the wolf was laughing at him. It felt like being aboard a rockslide as Finris laughed merrily. Avana too was snickering, making Killian feel even more annoyed and foolish.

Finally Finris said, "Forgive an old wolf for his jest. I am glad to see that Avana has chosen her life mate well. A strong warrior is what she needs. Though beware. She is a handful!"

"I can hear you, Finris!" Avana said, pretending to be injured by his words.

Killian grinned in spite of himself and replied, "I am well aware of that. I don't know how you put up with her."

"I survived with lots of patience, but if she ever gets too crazy, just stay out of the way and let her sort it out. She's a bit headstrong," Finris teased.

"Of course," Killian answered. He was starting to like and respect the old wolf. He was relieved that Finris had a sense of humor, though he seemed to be such a serious creature. It would be beneficial to have the wolf on his side.

Avana shook her head and sighed in exasperation. "You two are terrible. What am I going to do?"

Finris and Killian laughed in unison, causing Avana to roll her eyes. They were now on the edge of the Greenwood, and when they came into the open, Finris broke into a long lope that required all of the pair's concentration to stay on his back.

When they reached the edge of the valley, Finris stopped and allowed his passengers to dismount. "Speak to your soldiers,

Avana. I will wait here for you so I do not frighten them. It is good to be with you again," he growled, and nuzzled her gently.

Avana stroked his cheek saying, "I will come back for you soon, Father Wolf." Then she and Killian disappeared over the edge and down into the valley.

"Avana, you call him *Father*, and he calls you *Daughter*," Killian questioned in puzzlement as they walked down the valley. "I don't believe I quite understand."

Giving him a pensive look, remembering her time in the Wilds, Avana explained, "I never called on the Wild Wolves of the North for help, even though I had the horn. They found me as I wandered and took me in. They became my family when I had none. I pledged myself to them, and became part of the pack. Together we hunted down goblins and other evil creatures. I loved the Wild Wolves dearly, still do. My grandfather Aramis keeps in contact with them, so when I heard from him there was potential news of my father, I parted with the Wolves and made for Amaroth. It broke Finris's heart when I left, but he also knew that I must try and find my father."

Killian processed this information, carefully storing it in his memory. "No wonder you were a bit nervous when you called upon him. You were afraid he would be angry."

"Yes. Even though I left with his blessing, he was terribly sad. I wasn't sure how he would respond when I used the horn. It is not something I did lightly," Avana replied.

"I hope the soldiers are not afraid of Finris and his pack," Killian said after a moment. "It will be like fighting alongside a bedtime story for most of them."

Avana nodded in agreement. "I really don't know how they will react, but I hope that they will be strong and see the wisdom in calling on these allies."

Soon they reached the bottom of the vale and headed directly for their camp. Avana lost no time calling together the dwarves and men. She stood upon a hillock in the center of the valley and the soldiers gathered around her. When they all had assembled, she addressed the crowd. Avana projected her voice with a confident ring, and laid out everything to the warriors before her. When she spoke of the wolves, a murmur went through the crowd, but no one voiced any objections. She left nothing out, knowing that the truth would strengthen her credibility. Avana did not try to hide the fact that they were greatly outnumbered. Instead, she countered this by saying that with the help of the pack she felt sure they could rescue Halever. She ended by asking the men and dwarves if they would like to meet Finris. For a moment there was unrest in the group. Soon though an agreement was reached, and they called for Avana to introduce him. Avana faced the far edge of the valley, looking on the horizon of the ridge and let out a high clear whistle.

Like a gigantic ghost, Finris appeared with the sunlight shining from behind him, giving him a luminous glow. His white fur rippled in the breeze as he stood like a king. The effect made him look regal and big as a house, something out of a fairy tale, not a real creature of flesh and blood. A collective gasp went up from the crowd and some of the men stepped back in fear, whispering of witchcraft.

"Hold!" Avana commanded sternly and lo! The soldiers saw her also illuminated by the sun as she stood upon the hillock. She looked so tall and proud. Chestnut hair, brilliant as fire in the sunlight haloed her, and a fell light was in her eyes. She was regal as a queen, and those gathered before her truly understood who she was. The blood of kings and warriors ran through her veins. Surely they indeed could defeat the goblins and rescue Halever with her at their head.

The moment was broken when Finris began his descent into

the valley, loping gracefully toward them. Dwarf and man alike were left blinking, feeling as though they just witnessed something magnificent, something straight out of the past and coming to life before their eyes. Excitement rippled through them. A legend was in the making and they were part of it.

Avana joined Finris and with a mighty leap sprang upon his back. Drawing Stelenacht, she cried, "Some will not return from this fight, perhaps none of us will. Nonetheless, it is our duty to fight. Prepare for battle!" she thundered. The crowd roared in response to her words. With renewed vigor they began to prepare for the fight before them.

Killian was transfixed by what he just witnessed. Avana had come into her own—gone was the young girl of the past, and here, now, was a warrior to be reckoned with. Killian thought back to the prophecy from long ago. Though Avana might not realize it, she was beginning to fulfill it. The army prepared itself for battle, and by nightfall the camp was ready. By that time Fallon had returned with the promised wolves, and they gathered around the outside of the valley in a protective ring. With the pack keeping watch over the vale, Avana, Killian, Finris and Fallon made their final plans of attack. After deliberating some minor details, they decided that they would use the Thraicin River to access the goblins. The river's mouth was housed by a cave—large enough the wolves could enter it—and led almost directly to where Halever was held captive. The Thraicin was the main source of water for all creatures in the area, and it flowed all the way through the Wilds into Lonrach Lake. The cave would be heavily guarded, but with the help of Finris and his brethren, Avana felt sure they could punch through the goblins and rescue Halever.

Two things puzzled Killian. "How will you make it through the goblin line?" he asked Finris. "They will fill you with arrows before you could even get close."

Finris snorted contemptuously, "We are no ordinary wolves, Killian. Goblin arrows do not pierce our hides and it takes many strokes before a blade can bring us down. Do not worry about us."

Before they retired for the night, Killian asked Avana his second question. "If the wolves are not easily killed and you are friends with them, how did you come by the remarkable pelt you carry? It is obviously from one of them."

"You are correct, Killian," Avana said sadly. "The fur I carry is from Finris's mate, Rista."

"What?" Killian inhaled sharply.

Avana nodded and continued. "Many years ago, when my father was a young man, he and Finris were close friends. One day, Finris came to Caleb asking him for help. His mate Rista had gone hunting but never returned. He asked Caleb to help him look for her. Father agreed, and together, they searched the far reaches of the North. They found signs indicating an Ice Troll had taken her. Ice Trolls are the ancient nemesis of the Wild Wolves. They found Rista and the Ice Troll, but Rista was already dead. The Troll had killed her and taken her fur as a cloak. Together, Caleb and Finris fought and killed the Troll to avenge Rista. Finris was overwhelmed by grief and couldn't stand the sight of the fur. He bade Caleb take it, as the idea of it rotting away with the Troll was also abhorrent to him. My father kept it hidden away in a trunk with a few other valuables, buried at the base of a tree. When my family was killed, I took it. The skin was one of the reasons Finris believed my story and accepted me."

Killian gave Avana an appalled glance. "That's one of the saddest things I've ever heard. Does it not bother you knowing where the hide came from?"

"Yes, it does, but I wear it to honor Finris and Rista. Finris has been adamant that I keep it. I now think that he wants me to have it so I can bring about the prophecy."

Killian nodded. "It makes sense, I suppose. I doubt there are many furs like it. Come now, let us rest, for tomorrow we battle." With that, he kissed Avana, and they each went to their tents.

CHAPTER 15

MORNING CAME EARLY FOR THE CAMP. Armor was donned, and packs filled with food and water. It would be a two-hour march on foot as few of the horses could endure being close to the wolves. Some of the braver men agreed to ride the wild creatures; they were cautiously meeting their mounts.

Fallon approached Avana and asked, "Long has it been since we fought goblins together. Would you join me again today against our old foe?"

Avana looked up from the map laid out before her and replied, "It would be a great honor to fight alongside you, brother Fallon. Today we shall ride into battle together."

Soon the company was mustered and headed out. They rapidly reached the Thraicin River, and began to follow along its shores. This time there was no secrecy in their march. They were an army, despite their small numbers, and were headed for war.

When the cave was near, they broke into battle formation. Finris, Fallon, and the other wolves with riders were in the front, with the riderless wolves flanking them. Coming behind were the dwarves and men. It was agreed that once Halever was rescued, the army was to retreat even if the battle was going well for them. Their task was to rescue Halever, not to purge the goblin hole, and Avana wished for as few lives lost as possible. She and Killian also feared that if they charged too deeply into the goblin caverns, goblins from the surrounding areas would come and join the fray, thereby overwhelming their small army or blocking their escape.

Killian rode upon Finris, beside Avana on Fallon. Together, they formed the frontline of the battle. Both wore fitted armor that gleamed brightly in the sun. With swords at their sides and bows in hand, a bulging quiver on their backs completed their weaponry. The mouth of the river was now directly ahead of them and they readied their bows. In an unspoken agreement, the wolves broke into a stiff trot and plunged into the mouth of the cave.

Immediately the air was filled with the hiss of arrows from goblin bows. Avana and Killian sent their own arrows in reply. The whole of the cave was filled with goblins, but they retreated in fear when the wolves, snapping and growling ferociously, charged their ranks. The wolves were pelted endlessly, the arrows turning harmlessly off their hides and infuriating the goblins. Avana did her best to clear a path for Fallon with her bow, but the goblin numbers soon became too many. Avana drew her sword and began hacking at any goblin that tried to come at her from the sides.

Behind them the rest of the battalion, human and lupine alike, trickled into the cave, slowly driving the goblins back. Seeing their retreat, Fallon and Finris took a bold approach at the goblins. Letting out fearsome howls that reverberated off the walls, they leaped into the midst of the retreating creatures, crushing them with paw and fang. The other wolves soon joined in and spearheaded a drive through their enemy. The cavern narrowed alongside the river and the goblins found themselves bottlenecked in the tight space as they were driven farther back. Here they again attempted a stand against the army, sending dozens more arrows upon their attackers. Some of the men riding wolves were cut down, while others behind were injured. Fallon and Finris charged the goblins this time, leaping over the front line and into the middle of the goblin ranks. The goblins scattered from the angry wolves, some falling into the river as they struggled to escape.

Now the goblins were in full flight back to their main hole. The army cheered as they chased the foul creatures down the tunnel. Their joy was short-lived, however, as they came around the final bend into the open of the goblin hole, and a horde of the vile creatures swarmed to meet them. The cavern was a huge vault with many twisting tunnels leading into it. Almost the entire space was filled with goblins. Their war cries echoed angrily, creating a deafening din. *This does not look good at all*, Avana thought, her gaze roaming the vast space. She clung grimly to Fallon as he bucked and turned beneath her, fighting off the enemy. Avana's sword rang again and again as she defended the onslaught of blows. Desperately, she searched the great hall. There! Diagonally across from her was what she looked for—a low dark pit in the ground with heavy metal bars across the top. That would be the slave hole where Halever was being kept.

Crying out to Killian and Finris, Avana pointed to the hole. Drawing next to them she yelled over the clamor, "We will have to make a rush for it. Our entire army won't survive long in here. Call the archers to cover us!"

Killian relayed this to the men behind, and eight wolves joined Finris and Fallon.

"Are you ready?" Killian called out. "We will only get one chance to bull through!"

Avana laughed wildly and with a nudge to Fallon sprang away. Killian gave a shout, which Finris joined with a tremendous roar, and they threw themselves toward the slave pit. Behind them the archers kept up a steady stream of arrows, helping to clear a path for them. The wrathful wolves cleared any goblins that survived the archers. Avana's heart pounded as Fallon plowed through the goblins before them. Another leap and they would be at the side of the pit.

Suddenly, a giant goblin sprang up to face them. His head was nearly level with Avana's as she sat on Fallon's back. He carried an ugly battle-axe, and was tattooed with strange red markings from head to toe. The goblin backhanded Fallon, catching him off guard, and sent him stumbling nearly throwing Avana. At the same time, he raised his axe and brought down a stunning blow on Stelenacht as Avana tried to desperately to block him. Upon impact, Stelenacht pulsed a dazzling flash, momentarily blinding the goblin. This gave Fallon time to regain his footing and he rounded on the foul creature.

Avana ached from the impact, but still managed to deal a solid hit across the goblin's side. It bellowed angrily and again raised its axe to a ready position. That was as far as it got when three arrows, in rapid succession, pierced its chest. The goblin stumbled back and fell over dead, as Avana turned to see who saved her and Fallon. Behind them, upon Finris, Killian held his bow high and grinned broadly. He waved them on as a smile spread across Avana's face.

Within moments they were both at the edge of the pit, standing in front of the locked door. A complex padlock kept the entrance shut, and before Killian could begin to wonder how to open it, Stelenacht came slicing down upon the metal with a mighty clang. The lock burst asunder, and Avana hurriedly threw open the door. From below, two figures appeared stunned to see their rescuers. One of them was clearly Halever, Killian was ecstatic to see; the other was a gaunt, but fierce man. Killian reached down to help them out, turning his head toward Avana, her face now white as a ghost.

She trembled in disbelief. Behind her, the wolves snarled and fought against the goblins to allow her and Killian time to help the prisoners escape. But Avana was frozen. She couldn't believe it. The rough, shaggy form before her was her father!

Caleb's once golden hair was now darkened with streaks of gray in his curls, and he had a stubbly long beard. His clothes were tattered and stained, with bruises showing dark where the cloth was torn. Nonetheless, his eyes were still the intense gray-blue she remembered, and he still stood up proud though his body was thin and worn.

"Father!" she managed to croak out, at last, but this was all she could say.

Astonishment and reckoning blazed through Caleb's eyes as he beheld his grown daughter. He stepped forward to embrace her when a goblin came crashing down beside them.

Jumping to action, Caleb cried in a rolling voice, "Fly! We must fly from here or be destroyed!"

Without hesitation, he ran to the side of the nearest wolf and nimbly leapt upon it. Fallon was crouched next to Avana, and in a daze she managed to climb onto his back. She came back to reality when a goblin arrow nicked her forearm leaving a bright red trail of blood. This galvanized her back into action, and she brought Stelenacht down on the blade of a goblin that was hacking furiously at Fallon.

The return back to their warriors was much more difficult. The gap between them had almost doubled as the dwarves, the Guard, and rest of the pack had been pushed back almost to the tunnel. For at least part of the way back, they would be out of the range of their archers' protection. Avana knew their only hope was to keep pressing forward or else they'd be cut off and killed. Sheathing her sword for a moment, she switched to her bow and kept up a steady hail of arrows to allow Fallon a path.

Slight glancing blows to her legs were her biggest distraction, but she refused to let this break her concentration and continued her volley until they were near the tunnel. Only six wolves were left of the group that originally charged the slave pit. Two had been overcome by the goblins, and the remaining animals suffered slashes all over their bodies.

Fallon had a long welt across his muzzle where the goblin backhanded him, but he ignored the pain and snapped viciously at the goblins around him. Finally, Avana heard a telltale whistle of arrows overhead. They had reached the safety of the archers. With a last heave, Fallon sprang into the tunnel.

"Fall back to the outside!" Avana wailed.

Faster and faster the small army allowed themselves to be repelled back through the entrance of the tunnel. When the final company of warriors and wolves made it to the sunlit mouth of the cave, Avana and Fallon broke into the daylight, defending the rear to the last. They spilled out onto the green grass and took heart in the rays of the sun. Some of the fiercer goblins came after them, but the brightness of the sun worked against them. They recoiled from its light, shrinking back to the darkness of the cave. Now Avana's small army had the advantage. They easily dispatched any goblin brave enough to crawl out of the hole. At last no goblins were left, and the tired army gave a weary cry of victory. They turned from the riverside and with a heavy rear guard, began to head back to camp.

Avana's head was spinning. There, right in front of her, riding upon the big female named Alta, was her father. Avana could scarcely believe it. She had searched for years for Caleb, and now she had found him! Urging Fallon forward, she drew next to Alta and Caleb.

"I finally found you, Father!" Avana said in a voice full of joyous emotion. "I've spent almost my entire life searching for you. And here you are!" Tears gathered in her eyes as she finished speaking.

Caleb reached out for his daughter, enveloping her hand in his. His grip was sure, despite his hand being scarred and rough. "My wonderful daughter!" he said passionately. "I wasn't sure if you were dead or alive."

As he spoke, Killian with Halever on Finris also came up beside them.

"So you survived your captivity, old friend," Finris rumbled happily. "I am contented by your reunion with Avana. Though, you will have to share her with me. She is adopted into my pack now."

Smiling, Caleb let go of Avana's hand and slipped down from Alta's back. He walked over to Finris and laid his hand on the old wolf's coat.

"Thank you for taking care of her, Finris. I could think of no one better. I don't mind sharing her with you. I haven't been much of a father these last years," he ended wryly.

Avana jumped down from Fallon and ran to Caleb. "That's not your fault, Father! I know you did your best. You didn't give up, and because of that, I was able to find you!"

"Thank you for your kind words, daughter," Caleb answered, turning to her. "But I still feel responsible for leaving you alone."

Killian slid off of Finris to join Avana and Caleb. "Sir, no one blames you for what happened," he addressed Caleb. "Besides, you trained Avana well, so she was able to survive almost entirely on her own. She is strong and brave thanks to you." As he spoke this last part he slipped his arm around Avana.

Caleb eyed this action with a slight hint of disapproval. "Since when have you given your affections to a dwarf, Avana?"

Avana glared back at him. "Since he saved my life and helped me rescue you!"

Finris broke in with a growl. "Peace, Caleb! Killian is honorable and a nephew to Halfor. Even you could do no better for her."

Caleb looked abashed by this rebuke and apologized to Killian, who waved aside the apology and instead said courteously, "I understand your concerns. I am the one who should be asking for your forgiveness. I approached Avana without asking you first. Let me remedy that now. Caleb, son of Aramis, may I have permission to court your daughter, Avana?"

Impressed by Killian's thoughtfulness and manners, Caleb gave his consent to the request. After all, he trusted Finris's judgment, and what Avana had said was true. Avana beamed with pleasure at this, and Caleb realized his daughter was no longer the little girl he remembered. She was a young woman and that would take some getting used to.

Halever, aboard Finris, stayed silent while watching the entire exchange with a merry glint in his eyes. With a hearty laugh, he boomed from above them, "Sorry to interrupt this family reunion, but I haven't gotten a chance to thank you properly. You two saved my life! I doubt I can ever repay you, but I can promise if there is any help I can ever give you, be assured you shall have it."

Avana looked up at him and replied happily, "Think nothing of it, Prince Halever. No one should have to endure what you and my father have been through. You and he are the real heroes. I am grateful to simply find you alive."

"Oh, nonsense," Halever countered, "and please don't address me as *Prince*—I would be delighted to call you my friend, and my friends only call me Halever."

"All right then . . . Halever," Avana said with a slight hesitation. "Now I suppose you both want to hear the story of how we found you?"

Caleb and Halever both eagerly called for the tale and listened with keen interest. Avana started with her life back when

Caleb had first been abducted, and then with Killian's help, brought the story to the present. They finished by explaining the disturbing rise in goblin attacks and their course of action after Halever's kidnapping.

When the tale concluded, Avana noticed her father looked deeply troubled. "What's wrong, Father?"

Caleb sighed and shook his head in chagrin. "Something I failed to mention earlier and should have . . . I got too caught up in finding you again. You were right to assume something is going on with the goblins. They are planning for war."

"For war?" Killian nearly stumbled in surprise. "But the goblins were virtually destroyed in the Great War years ago. I know their numbers have increased, but surely not enough to launch a full scale attack on the nations of Arda!"

"Yes, I'm afraid it is so. The goblin chieftain, Garzvahl himself, told me of his plans as he gloated over me when he learned Halever had been captured. You see, Garzvahl intended to capture as many important leaders from each race as he could. Then, with his army behind him, he planned to take Amaroth, and from there invade the Tiered Mountain. Then, eventually, lay siege to the elves. By seizing Halever and me, he had a good start to his scheme. Garzvahl knew there would be an attempt to rescue Halever, and he hoped Commander Ruskin himself would come. However, a famous up and coming captain like you, Avana, would not be a bad prize either. Unfortunately for Garzvahl, we escaped his grasp. That's not the worst of it, though. The goblins have created a new breed of fighters that are not affected by the sun. They also have formed an alliance with an ancient foe, one I thought no longer existed: the Ice Trolls."

At this, Finris gave such a ferocious growl that even Caleb trembled. "Ice Trolls, you say?" Finris vibrated with animosity. "Surely there are only a few left of those treacherous creatures."

Caleb shook his head. "I'm sorry, old friend. It seems Garz-vahl has found a colony of Trolls in the farthest reaches of the North, where even your kind does not care to wander. I know they are a good bit fewer than a thousand, but even a hundred Ice Trolls are a serious threat to the peoples of Arda."

"This is very dire news indeed," Halever said pensively. "I believe we may need to call a council of the races—man, dwarf, and elf—as this could be the start of another great war."

"And wolf!" Finris interjected heatedly.

Halever replied, "Pardon me, Finris, and wolf! We will be glad to have your input. I know the Ice Trolls have long been your enemy."

"I think I agree with you, Halever," Caleb said with a resigned look. "I myself would go to the elves if all present think this is a wise course of action."

The group readily concurred with Caleb, and Halever turned to Killian. "Would you come and explain everything to my father? I want to make sure he hears all the facts correctly, as I am not sure I have all the information to do so."

"Assuredly," Killian replied quickly. "Only, I wish for Avana to come with me."

Halever nodded enthusiastically, "It would make sense to have an envoy from Amaroth accompany you. What say you, Avana?"

"As long as Commander Ruskin approves, I would be honored to go." Avana smiled up at Halever.

"Well, then, I shall personally ask for you," Halever said. "Ruskin can hardly afford to anger a prince." The last part was spoken with a teasing wink, adding a bit of mirth to the dark mood of the company.

The rest of the march back to camp was spent detailing the logistics of what it would take to host a council of the races. When they reached the valley, Avana realized she was utterly exhausted from the day's events. The stress of battle, and the relief she experienced in freeing her father, had made for an emotional ride. A part of her still found it hard to believe she was walking with her father again. They had succeeded in rescuing Halever, and at the same time found Caleb. It was almost too much, and Avana had tears in her eyes as she looked upon the peaceful valley before her. Killian walked up behind her and embraced her.

"All will be well," he said simply, and for the second time in many years, Avana cried. This time, though, they were tears of joy.

Word that the other rescued prisoner was the famed Ranger Caleb quickly spread through the camp. There was much celebration that night over the safe return of Halever and Caleb. Though they rejoiced, they also made preparations to break camp and head for home. The sooner they left, the better, for there was always a lingering possibility the goblins would find their camp and attack.

CHAPTER 16

AVANA SPENT THE JOURNEY BACK TO AMAROTH renewing her relationship with her father. He in turn came to know her and her comrades. He found he had much in common with Svengale and the two quickly became friends. Avana also enjoyed getting to know Halever. His green eyes and long red beard flashed when he laughed, which was often, as he was swift to merrymaking. His eyes were also shrewd in their assessment of any situation. Avana felt that he sometimes knew her better than she knew herself; he was that astute in his evaluations. Killian and Halever spent a great deal of time together acting almost as brothers. To her surprise, Avana was a bit jealous of having to share Killian, but this feeling soon passed.

When they reached Amaroth, the company was greeted with great joy and fanfare from the rest of the Guard. Caleb stopped in the gateway and rested a hand on the great stone arches. His eyes misted over briefly. The last time he was here was with his wife, Aileen. So much had changed since then. He looked at Avana, striding ahead of him into the city. *She was so much like her mother*, he thought. He felt a swell of pride for his daughter as he saw her greeted warmly by the citizens of Amaroth, who clearly loved and respected her. Avana was everything he had hoped she would be, and he was mightily proud to be her father.

Commander Ruskin and Captain Grayson welcomed the

pair graciously. Grayson lost no time in reaching out to Caleb to apologize for his temper and for arguing all those years before. Caleb was elated to see Grayson, and he also begged for his forgiveness for his own stubborn hotheadedness. The two men quickly reconciled and their old friendship was rekindled. Halever immediately requested that Avana come with Killian as a representative of Amaroth to the dwarven court. Ruskin readily agreed to this request when he heard the news Caleb brought from the goblins.

Ruskin and Grayson were disturbed by the events that transpired. The news of impending war brought great unease to the two leaders. Commander Ruskin knew he needed to fortify the city for battle. Amaroth had not seen war in hundreds of years. He realized the citizens were ill-prepared for an attack, and it would take an enormous amount of work to organize them. His main concern, though, was how the citizens could escape the city if the fight went ill. Ruskin decided that when Halfor came to the council, he would ask him for permission to evacuate the citizens of Amaroth to the stronghold of the Tiered Mountain, should war come upon them. Amaroth was full of families with many children who needed to be kept out of harm's way.

Caleb, Avana, Killian, and Halever rested only for a day before preparing again for their respective journeys. Something was bothering Avana though. She approached her father with her query. "Father, I have been carrying your sword ever since you were kidnapped, and I believe it's time to return it to you." There was resignation in her voice as she held Stelenacht out to him.

Caleb looked at her for a long moment, "No, daughter, it is no longer mine. It belongs wholly to you now. You have earned the right to keep it. Besides, the elven king Valanter owes me a favor. I shall take a new blade for the battle to come, though I wish I never had to fight again." With these words he gently curled her fingers back around the scabbard and closed his hands over hers. "You may need the sword in the days ahead. You have done well with it. It would be unwise to break such a bond."

"Thank you, Father. It will never leave my side and will always remind me of you, just as it has all these years," Avana replied with a grateful smile.

The following day Caleb was ready to begin his journey to the Greenwood where the elves lived in the farthest southern parts. It had been more than thirty years since he last visited the elven realm, and he hoped he could still remember how to find their chief citadel, Mirava. He bid his goodbyes to his friends and, last of all, to Avana.

Hugging her tightly he said, "We shall soon meet again, fair daughter. Be strong and know that your father loves you!" With that he pulled away and swung up onto his horse. Waving farewell, he trotted through the city gates and onto the road that led through the Wilds.

Avana's heart was heavy as she watched her father ride away. She had just found him and now they were separated again. Part of her longed to be at his side, but she knew her duty was to go to the Tiered Mountain with Killian. For the past three years, she hoped for an opportunity to do so, and she needed to make the most of this chance.

Avana, Killian, Halever and the rest of the dwarves set off for the Tiered Mountain three days later. Their journey was much shorter than Caleb's. The Cascade Mountains were beautiful, and as they traveled deeper into their reaches, Avana was in awe of the sight. Snow-capped peaks tumbled down to sharp crevasses, but not all of the mountains were uninhabitable. The peaks hid deep rolling valleys filled with pine trees and spacious green meadows that stretched across the arms of the mountains. Hidden in the recesses of the Cascades stood the Tiered Mountain. It twisted and curved so dramatically that it gave the impression of multiple peaks stacked on top of one another, hence its name. This great fortress was where the dwarves made their home in massive caverns and halls far beneath the mountain.

As they drew near the Mountain, the road leveled out and became broad and well paved, evidence that they were entering the reaches of the dwarven kingdom. One side of the Tiered Mountain was rocky and barren, while the other had a river rushing down it and held more of the meadows they had seen previously. The Mountain's entrance was an enormous gateway carved intricately into the rock with many columns of pillars. The stonework was plated entirely with gold, making the entry shine brilliantly in the sun.

Avana was absolutely stunned by the beauty of the dwarves' home. When they reached the main causeway, she was even more startled to realize the towering lampposts that lined the road appeared to be made of solid gold. Even the stones that served as pavement were all semi-precious jewels. She had heard tales of the dwarves' wealth, but nothing could have prepared her for this.

Dwarves streamed from the Mountain to welcome and celebrate Halever's safe return. Their rough voices filled the air with gladness and elation over their prince's homecoming. Trumpets sounded and from somewhere deep in the Mountain a drum boomed a low, welcoming chorus. Happy dwarves seeking to greet their lost prince enveloped the group. Halever and Killian were embraced and applauded many times over. Avana, however, was regarded with a slight degree of suspicion, though several handshakes were offered to her.

Finally, they made it into the Mountain where Avana was even more amazed at the city before her. The roof was vaulted so high above her that she could not see the ceiling, and yet it was brilliantly lit up in its entirety. Huge murals of dwarven history lined the walls and watched over the city below them. The city itself was an impressive sight. Houses built of the finest marble with delicate detailing lined every street. Even the smallest buildings seemed ornately decorated and polished to a gleam.

"What do you think of my home, Avana?" Killian asked as he watched her take it all in.

"It is breathtaking, Killian. I can't believe it's real! It seems impossible, but I'm looking right at it. I see now why you wished me to visit with you."

Killian took her hand as they wound their way through the city streets to the king's court. The palace was heavily guarded, but the group was quickly let through with shouts of joy at the sight of Halever. They were hastily ushered into the throne room full of brightly dressed courtiers where a large dwarf sat on a richly decorated chair, situated on a tall dais. The king wore a light coat of chain mail over a dark green shirt with deep blue pants and heavy boots. A thick gold band studded with diamonds and rubies encircled his head, and his rust colored beard fell in neat braided plaits down to his knees. Green eyes that matched Halever's widened in surprise as the trio entered the room, leaving no doubt that this was the dwarven king, Halfor.

Instantly, he sprang to his feet, and with a nimbleness that belied his girth, he rushed to embrace his son. Halever raced toward the king and they hugged with a fierceness that made Avana ache for her own father.

Holding Halever at arm's-length, Halfor boomed in a gravelly voice, "You are alive, my son! Your mother and I feared we would never see you again."

"I am alive and well, Father! Namely thanks to cousin Killian and Captain Avana. It was their initiative and swordcraft that rescued me. I owe them a great debt," Halever replied happily.

Turning from Halever, Halfor surveyed Killian and Avana while a large smile spread across his face. "Thank you for saving Halever. Killian, I knew that you were the dwarf for the job, and I have heard much sung in your praises, Avana. I am sure you were just as valuable in the rescue. I wish to honor you both. Tomorrow, a feast will be held to celebrate."

"Father!" Halever broke in. "he time of celebration must wait. We bring most disturbing news that I fear should take precedence over merriment."

Halfor looked annoyed and said, "What, pray tell, are such dire tidings that can detain a feast?"

"Commander Ruskin wishes to hold a council of the races—men, dwarves, and·elves. We have learned the goblins are preparing to wage war against us," Halever replied quietly.

A collective gasp went up from the courtiers at this announcement. The joy that so recently covered Halfor's face was erased by these words, and instead he looked tired and resigned. "Come, let us retire to one of my council chambers. I will call the captains to join us." With a wave of his hand he dismissed the courtiers from the throne room, and the three trailed him to a side chamber. There they sat around a table that Avana found to be a bit low for her comfort, but she did not complain. Once the captains of the army were assembled, Killian and Avana filled everyone in on all that happened and the information Caleb acquired. Halfor was extremely pleased to hear of Caleb's rescue and congratulated Avana on finding her father. He did not seem entirely surprised about the goblins' plans. At length he said, "I had suspicions that this was coming, ever since the goblin uprisings started. I will go to the council, though I already know what our course of action must be. We will prepare for battle."

More was discussed on the matter, and they deliberated late

into the afternoon. As evening drew near, Avana found that she couldn't help herself and a long yawn escaped her. Halfor's quick eyes noticed her tiredness and he said, "Forgive my poor manners, dear girl! You are weary from your long travels and dwarves can talk without rest for great lengths of time. Killian, take her and find food and lodging for you both. Tomorrow we shall still break bread together, but it will not be the celebration I had hoped for. Peace and goodnight to you."

Killian replied, "We shall stay with my family tonight. My mother would never forgive me if we did otherwise." Leading Avana to a house just outside of the palace, Killian knocked on a heavily carved wooden door. It swung open to reveal a husband and wife. She shrieked in delight at the sight of Killian. "You are home at last!" the lovely dwarf woman cried. Her thick brown hair hung in platelets down her back, and she wore a sky blue dress accented with tiny mirrors sewn into the seams. She reached out and threw her arms around Killian, sending light dancing across the floor from the mirrors.

Behind her, Killian's father smiled warmly at the reunion. "Welcome back, son. We did not expect to see you so soon, though news had reached us of Halever's rescue." Killian's father Kalmar was quite similar in stature and features to his brother Halfor. But where his brother's hair was red, Kalmar's was dark. In likeness, they had the same green eyes and a beard that hung to their waist.

Killian released his mother and directed his attention toward Avana, who was standing awkwardly in the doorway. "Avana, this is my mother, Zyphereth, and my father, Kalmar," and to his parents he said, "This is Avana, daughter of Caleb, who we found and rescued along with Halever. I have wished for you to meet her for some time."

Zyphereth enveloped Avana in a warm embrace. "So this

is the lovely young lady who has stolen the heart of my son! I am pleased to meet you." Holding Avana away from her for a moment, she continued, "My, you are a pretty thing! And you have that same wild glint to your eyes as your father. No wonder Killian is smitten."

Avana blushed, taken aback by Zyphereth's words, and turned even pinker when instead of being abashed, Killian simply laughed at his mother.

Avana finally stammered, as Killian's mother released her, "It's very nice to meet you Zyphereth and you, too, Kalmar. You have a fine son whom I am grateful to call my friend. I love him very much."

"Well, you seem to be a good match for him, Avana," Kalmar replied, taking her by the arm and leading her into the house. "Let us dine together and you both can tell us your story. We are anxious to hear it."

They ate a hearty meal of fish and vegetables with slices of thick bread. Avana rarely drank, but she found that the thick, honeyed mead the dwarves served with dinner was not too strong for her. Instead, the mead filled her with pleasing warmth and drove the weariness from her bones. Relaxed and quite full, Avana leaned back in her chair and watched Killian interact with his family. She had almost forgotten what home felt like, and this brought back old memories. She had failed to recall the feeling of security and love for so long that she hadn't realized it was missing from her life until this moment. Inside her, emotions stirred and she longed for the day when she could settle down and have a family again. Perhaps when this was all over she would get her wish.

Presently, they retired to a cozy living room where a crackling fire lit the hearth with a cheerful light. Kalmar settled down with a pipe in his hand, and soon the pleasant smell of its smoke permeated the room. Avana sat on a low couch next to Killian and leaned upon his shoulder. The voices of the family rose and fell as they continued to catch up. Avana found herself drifting in and out of slumber as she listened. Eventually she drifted off completely. Much later she woke to strong arms around her carrying her to bed. She sleepily looked up to see Killian's kind smile as he lowered her gently onto a soft quilt. He tucked her in, and with a whisper of goodnight and a kiss on her forehead, he retired to his own room. Avana quickly slipped back into her dreams and rested without a care for the first time in months.

She awoke the next morning to the delightful smell of bacon frying. She noticed there was also a new change of clothes thoughtfully laid out on a chair across from the bed. It was a blue dress made out of the same material and style as what Zyphereth had worn the night before. Avana was worried at first that it would not fit her, but when she held it up in front of the mirror, she knew she was mistaken. She slipped the dress on and was surprised at the change it brought over her. She was beautiful! Avana couldn't remember the last time she had worn a real dress. She felt out of place, yet it was so lovely that she couldn't help but admire herself. Her one concession to this normal attire was to belt her knives around her waist, which accentuated her figure while adding an air of boldness.

Gliding silently down the hall, she made her way to the kitchen where Zyphereth stood in front of a stove with a checkered apron pulled over her skirt. When she turned and saw Avana she let out a happy cry of delight. "I knew that would be perfect for you! I had the seamstress make you one like mine because I was sure it would set off your eyes. Besides, you will need something appropriate to wear when you go before the king. Battle dress is fine for every day, if that's what you like, but the king plans to decorate you. It wouldn't be right to not have you properly attired."

She proffered a steaming plate of hotcakes and bacon, which Avana gratefully accepted. As Avana set the plate down, she looked up to find Killian staring at her from the hallway.

"What? Did I forget to comb my hair again?" Avana teased him.

Killian was speechless as he continued to stare at her. He walked toward her, as if drawn by a string, until he stood only a few feet from where she sat at the table. "You're . . . beautiful," he finally managed. "I've never . . . I've never seen you in a dress before!"

Avana eyed him with a cool gaze. "Ladies do wear them, you know," she added a wink as she watched Killian struggle to pull up a chair beside her. Zyphereth laughed merrily over her son's tongue-tiedness and brought him a plate of hotcakes and bacon. Soon, she too settled down with a plate and they ate heartily. It wasn't until after breakfast that Killian's stunned expression began to wear off.

Kalmar had already left in the early hours of the morning to consult with his brother, Halfor. After their meal was finished, Killian and Avana went back to the palace to join him. Again they went long into the afternoon with their planning. If war was inevitable, Halfor knew Commander Ruskin would ask him to shelter the folk of Amaroth. Already he began to make arrangements for the people to take refuge there, and he set aside food from his stores for them.

Halfor ended deliberations an hour before the evening meal. A small celebration was to be held that night to honor Avana and Killian for rescuing his son. Once they were excused from Halfor's chamber, Killian took Avana's hand and led her through the city.

"I've something I wish to show you," he said secretively, and didn't say more. When they drew to the edge of the city, he asked her to close her eyes. Still holding her hand, he led her through many twists and turns. Avana felt that they were going up, but this was all she could tell. Finally, she sensed a light breeze washing over them. She guessed they were somewhere on the mountainside.

"You can open your eyes now, Avana," Killian spoke with a smile in his voice. Avana opened her eyes and gave a small gasp in surprise. They were standing on a large terrace paved with flagstones of green marble. Around the edges grew a lovely garden with dozens of flowers flowing cheerfully down the mountainside. Steps made of the same green stone wound down to a wide green meadow ringed by tall cedar trees. The view was breathtaking. Avana spun to face Killian. "It's absolutely amazing! I never imagined such a place existed!" she cried dreamily.

Killian's eyes sparked happily. "I'm glad you like it because it's yours. Well, ours," he amended, "If you agree to be my wife, this is where we will live."

Avana couldn't help herself and let out a happy laugh, "It's absolutely perfect. I would be glad to live here with you. But how did you come by it?"

"Remember when Halever asked if there was anything he could ever do for us? This was my request. He was more than happy to give this land to me. If we both survive the coming battle, I intend to build a house recessed into the mountain and this shall be the porch. How does that sound to you?" Killian replied, gesturing to the rock face behind them.

"I think that would be excellent!" Avana beamed. With that, the two descended into the meadow below and spent the next few minutes exploring the large area. Soon though, they had to leave and return to the king's celebration.

Avana's heart sang as she walked back to the feast awaiting them. It seemed the home she had so recently been longing for was now hers for the taking. As they entered the hall where the meal was held, a great thunder of applause came from those seated around the room. Halfor boomed from the head of the table, "Welcome, my honored guests!" addressing Avana and Killian. To the dwarves sitting around him he announced, "May I present Avana, daughter of Caleb, and Killian, son of Kalmar, the two brave warriors who rescued Halever."

Applause chorused up again with scattered shouts of approval. "Draw near, you two," Halfor commanded. "Cassia and I thank you for the return of our son." He gestured to the pretty dwarf woman at his side. Avana and Killian approached the king's side. Standing up from the table, Halfor waved two servants over bearing gifts as he declared, "Avana, Captain of the Guard of Amaroth, I present you with a scabbard made of bright silver for your sword, Stelenacht. I name you dwarf friend for your acts of bravery and courage. May your blade never grow dull and your arm ever be strong!"

Turning to Killian he said, "Killian, my nephew, I present you with a new bow and quiver. It is reinforced with many magic wards. As long as you hold it, I do not think it will ever fail its mark. May your arrows never be dull and your arm ever be strong!"

With that, he embraced them both and gestured for them to sit next to him as more applause rose from the dwarves. Sitting alongside the king, they dined on many courses of rich food. This was the most elaborate banquet Avana had ever attended, but she felt at ease with Killian at her side and Halfor's kindness to her. The king treated her like the high-born lady her heritage demanded, yet did so without coming across patronizing as he did so. Much laughter and joy made the dinner a lively affair. Though it was small compared to what Halfor initially wanted, the celebration truly was one of thanksgiving and honor. When the last toasts were made and dessert eaten, the dwarves bid their farewells and goodnights to the king and his honorees.

Avana and Killian thanked Halfor for his gifts and for the evening. Then they retired for the night. When they returned to the palace the next day, they found it in an uproar. A message had come to the mountain from Caleb. It read:

To Halfor, Halever, Killian, and My Daughter, Avana,

I reached Valanter's courts and have persuaded him to our cause. I am nearly too late, however. The elves report that Garzvahl has mustered his forces in the North and is making plans to march on Amaroth. His armies are nearly forty thousand strong, counting the Ice Trolls. I fear this may be the end of us all. I have contacted my father, Aramis. We will have the aid of the Rangers though their numbers are few. Return to Amaroth as soon as you receive this. I also have let Commander Ruskin know of the danger. Alert Finris to the need at hand; he will gather all the free Wolf packs of the North to fight alongside us. Halfor, I would advise you to not send your full force to Amaroth. If we lose the city, we will be driven back to your mountain and it will need defending. Also, I would ask permission for the people of Amaroth to evacuate to the mountain. I hope to see you all soon.

Faithfully yours,
Caleb

Avana and Killian were dismayed by this news. Halfor barely had time to speak to them as he hastened his battle preparations. His army consisted of fifteen thousand able bodied dwarves, but in accordance with Caleb's word, he decided to leave five thousand to guard the Tiered Mountain. Halfor, too, realized the mountain might be the place where a last stand could be made. Their city was in a frenzy as they began to set up barricades along the road and prepare the soldiers for the fight ahead. Halfor bid Killian and Avana to leave for Amaroth that day with the first thousand dwarf soldiers who were always prepared for times such as this. Quickly they packed their gear and found themselves on the road to Amaroth before noon.

CHAPTER 17

THEY MARCHED AT A FAST PACE, pushing on late into the night. Keeping up the double time speed, they returned to Amaroth in half the normal span it took to reach the city. As they approached, they encountered hundreds of citizens fleeing to the Tiered Mountain. Amaroth itself was abuzz in preparation for the coming battle along with the evacuation to Halfor's kingdom. Any strong men from the surrounding area were being recruited to join Amaroth's army. Families who lived along Lonrach Lake fled to the city, and while the women and children were urged to go on to the Tiered Mountain, all the men were asked to stay and fight. Amaroth's own army from the Guard was only four thousand strong, but with the addition of locals, their ranks swelled to roughly fifty-five hundred.

Avana desperately hoped the elves would help even out their odds against the goblins. However, she feared that, even with their help, it would not be enough. She summoned Finris and caught him up on everything she knew. He promised to muster as many wolves as he could. This would be the greatest gathering of the packs since the times of the kings of old. What she asked would not be taken lightly by the wild Northern packs, but he was sure they would come to her aid.

Commander Ruskin kept Avana busy organizing the Guard. He also called on Killian to be his lead for the archers. Two days after Avana and Killian reached the city, Halfor and Halever, with the dwarf army at their backs, marched into Amaroth. Their soldiers camped along the slopes, causing the mountain to look like it was covered in stars when their fires were lit at night. Ruskin invited the dwarf royalty to his meetings as they planned their strategy. Garzvahl could attack at any time and Ruskin was afraid the battle would start before the elves could reach them. In a bold move, Commander Ruskin named Avana his second in command, and Captain Grayson her lieutenant.

Though she was grateful for the honor, Avana realized that if Ruskin were to perish in the fight ahead, the command of the entire Guard would fall to her. That thought was frightening, and Avana thrust it away from her, not wishing to acknowledge such a possibility. Instead, she took comfort in knowing Grayson and Killian would be alongside her should anything go wrong.

Two more days of frantic preparation passed while mounting tension built throughout the city. As the sun rose on the third day, the sound of howling, fierce and wild, descended over the city. Man and dwarf alike scrambled for their weapons and looked over the walls of the town to see what approached. A white sea of wolves raced across the hills toward the city and a deep horn blast echoed from Amaroth in response to their baying.

Avana dashed to the gates with Killian and Grayson hot on her heels. There, she was met by panting Finris and Fallon. Finris spoke after regaining his breath, "The goblins are coming! They were close behind, driving us on. We outpaced them, but they are no more than a few hours' march away. Ready yourselves for battle! I have assembled as many wolves as would come. Packs from all reaches of the Wilds and the North, around two thousand in all. We are considerably outnumbered. There are many more than forty thousand goblins approaching, and the Ice Trolls carry great bows with them like the ones they made in the old days. A single arrow from their quiver can easily pin a Northern Wolf to the ground. We will be hard pressed in this fight," he ended solemnly.

Avana laid a hand on Finris's muzzle and quietly replied, "If it comes to the end, I shall be proud to have spent it fighting beside you, Father Wolf. I will never forget what you have done for me."

Finris nuzzled her gently, whining softly. Fallon too butted his nose up against her. Putting aside her worries, Avana hugged each in turn. Wheeling back around to face the city, she brought her horn to her lips and blew a long blast to signal Amaroth that the goblins were coming. From along the walls answering horns rang out as shouts rose up carrying the news. Armor and chain mail were quickly donned while archers began to take their positions along the ramparts of Amaroth.

The dwarf army marched through the city and took up their station outside. Their helmets glittered in blue and gold. The heavy rectangular shields they carried were embossed with Halfor's gold star on midnight blue backing. The ground surrounding the road leading into the city had dozens of deep trenches that had been dug and filled with sharp stakes. These were carefully covered over to look like the rest of the land. The dwarves chose to take up the location between the trenches and Lonrach Lake. Behind them the Guard of Amaroth covered the road, mingling with the Wolves of the North.

Inside Amaroth, Commander Ruskin hastily finished organizing the blockades within each district. He knew if they were pushed back into the city, they must have their defenses ready. He ordered as much fresh water as possible be drawn and stored in barrels so it was available to the infirmaries should they be cut off from the main wells. The city's stores were full with many months of supplies, but Ruskin was adamant they were checked and rechecked to ensure everything was ready for the worst possible scenario.

The whole countryside held its breath in extreme anxiety as they waited for the first goblins to appear over the horizon. At noon the great watch horn of Amaroth was blown to signal the sighting of the enemy. The goblins marched in never-ending dark lines across the hills toward Amaroth. They sang a hideous chant as they tramped incessantly forward carrying black banners before them. Scattered among their ranks were gigantic Ice Trolls. Standing tall as a house with legs like tree trunks, they made even the goblins nervous with their presence. Blueish gray skin with bulls' horns sprouting from their heads, and saber fangs made them terrifying. Clad in ugly black armor, they carried enormous bows and double headed battle-axes engraved with profane spells. Skulls hung from their belts, while their shields were covered in the hides of their victims.

Avana trembled in spite of herself. She buried her hand in Finris's fur, giving way to her fears momentarily. *What hope did we have in defeating such a force?* she wondered. Where were the elves and her father? Surely they must be close.

Sensing her fright, Finris nudged her gently. "Courage, dear one. Have we not fought against terrible odds before? Is it not our duty to challenge the dark?"

Leaning thankfully upon Finris, Avana answered, "Yes. You are right. It just seems impossible."

"You are the very definition of the impossible coming true, Avana," Finris laughed. "Now you have a purpose and a destiny to fulfill. Let us ride together to death and glory."

Feeling comforted, Avana's resolve was strengthened. She sprang lightly upon Finris's back and they trotted over to Killian who was already sitting astride Fallon. Together they made their way to the front lines. A steely anger hardened inside Avana as she watched the approaching goblins. All of the sadness, pain, and loneliness she carried for so long welled up into a fiery resolve that burned with an unquenchable thirst.

Drawing Stelenacht from its sheath, she turned Finris toward her troops and addressed them with a proud voice, "Today we fight! Today we die! Not one goblin shall enter the city! We will spill every drop of our blood before that will happen. We fight for those we love. We will not let them down." With a final cry she yelled, "For death and glory!"

A thunderous roar emanated from the troops in answer to her words. The red pennant with the gold dragon snapped crisply in the wind. The horn of Amaroth sounded again deep and rolling. The gates of the city opened, and Commander Ruskin with Captain Grayson and fifteen hundred soldiers rode out along the road to meet the coming enemy. Dozens of sonorous horns too sounded from the dwarf army as Halfor rode to their front on a shaggy, stout war pony flanked by Halever.

Across from them the goblin line had stopped at the sound of the horns. Even their chanting had ceased, leaving in its place an eerie silence even more frightening than their voices. Suddenly an Ice Troll raised a dark curling horn with many foul incantations etched into the sides and blew a mighty blast. Its raucous call reverberated over the ranks of goblins and in response they sent up a dreadful yell. With that, they drew their weapons and began to race toward the waiting army.

Coming alongside Killian, Avana turned to him and said as the enemy came rushing toward them, "You have my love, Killian. Will you fight at my side in perhaps our last battle? I can think of no one else I would rather have with me."

"It would be the highest honor I could think of, Avana," Killian replied huskily. "Let us now ride, for the enemy is upon us!"

With dreadful howls, Finris and Fallon leapt forward in

unison toward the oncoming tide of goblins. Flanked on either side were many men and dwarves, also riding on the back of wolves, and carrying bows. As their adversaries came into range, they let loose a terrific volley of arrows, effectively mowing down the front line of the goblins. Nonetheless, the rest of the horde continued to press on in spite of the deadly hail raining down on them. Now the goblins were almost face to face with them. The riders drew their swords. The two sides clashed together with a terrible shrieking of metal. The screeching and cursing of goblins, men, and dwarves mingled with the growling of the wolves, sending up a terrific clamor.

Stelenacht flared a brilliant blue in Avana's hand as she battled the swarms of goblins seeking to overwhelm her. The sword reflected her mood as she mowed an opening before her. Both Avana and Finris were filled with a powerful bloodlust and none could stand before them. Abruptly an Ice Troll rose up in their path. Finris snarled in terrible wrath and hatred for this creature, his greatest enemy. Drawing himself together he made a mighty leap and succeeded in knocking the Troll backwards. As the Troll staggered to regain its balance, Avana dealt a fierce blow with Stelenacht to the Troll's back, the creature bellowing in pain and anger. Finding its balance again, the Troll brought its axe down on Stelenacht, causing sparks to fly from the blade. Now fully roused to anger, the beast began to rain down a barrage of lightning quick thrusts with the axe. Finris found he had to give ground just to avoid the Troll as it battered them mercilessly.

Suddenly, Killian and Fallon appeared next to them. Killian's bow sang as he put an arrow into the eye of the Troll, the creature roaring in agony and clawing its wounded eye. Angrily it lunged forward, and swinging its axe indiscriminately, the Troll managed to unseat Killian with a glancing hit. Killian went rolling beneath Fallon's legs. Avana yelled in distress when she saw Killian fall. Across the plains from them, a horn blasted and Commander Ruskin's riders charged into the fray, momentarily causing the Ice Troll to turn and face the oncoming force. This was enough distraction for Avana to deliver the Troll a deadly blow. For a moment it swayed, then came crashing down, dead.

Worried, Avana spun toward Killian. She found him covered in mud, pulling himself off the ground and climbing onto Fallon's back again. "You can't get rid of me that easily!" He laughed roguishly at her expression and urged Fallon back into the battle.

Avana let out a full laugh and with Finris launched after Killian and Fallon. The appearance of Commander Ruskin and his horsemen had driven the goblins toward the pits the men had dug. As the riders pressed onward, the goblins and Trolls began falling through the ground, sending pandemonium through their ranks. Dwarves had joined the fray and began to attack goblins from the other side.

Goblins were now fighting on three different fronts: Commander Ruskin on the left side with his horsemen; Avana, Killian, and the wolves in the middle; and Halfor and the dwarves on the right. Man, dwarf, and wolf strove mightily against the enemy. Over and over they were pushed back, only to rally and press forward again. They mowed down the goblins fearlessly, but no matter how many they killed, another goblin rose to take the last one's place. Avana felt herself tire. She could feel the slowed movements of Finris beneath her. She knew they could not keep up their line much longer. Their forces exhausted, no one was there to relieve them.

Finally, Avana sounded her horn to signal the wolves to begin their retreat to the city. She was answered by horns from the Guard and the dwarves. Slowly, they allowed themselves to be pushed back toward the city walls. Dusk was beginning to fall and watch fires were being lit on the ramparts causing the city to light up with an angry glow. Commander Ruskin and his horsemen began to withdraw toward Avana and the wolf fighters. Unexpectedly, the goblins rallied and made a rush for the commander, overwhelming the force. Suddenly, Ruskin found himself and his group surrounded by goblins. Killian was first to notice their plight and called out to Avana, directing her attention to the beleaguered riders.

Now the goblins were pressing their advantage and they swarmed around the horsemen, causing them to retreat into a tight knot. It was evident the riders would soon be overcome. Avana gave another blast on her horn and the wolves regrouped. They pressed boldly toward the horsemen with as much haste as possible. Seeing their approach, the Ice Trolls began a deadly volley of arrows upon Avana's ranks. All around her, wolves fell as the arrows found their targets. Ahead of them Avana saw Ruskin's force also being cut down. Captain Grayson fought the tide with violent strokes trying to press through the goblins, but made little headway.

With a fierce yell, Commander Ruskin united his now small band of soldiers and made a headlong rush toward the wolves. Before he could reach them, two Ice Trolls intercepted him. In a panic his horse reared up, lashing out with its hooves kicking one of the Trolls. But its hooves never touched ground again. Instead, the other Troll clubbed the horse with a heavy mace, sending both horse and rider flying. Ruskin was thrown clear, but struggled to stand, his leg broken from the terrible fall. The goblins around him began to beat him down mercilessly with their blades. Grayson was separated from Ruskin by the Trolls, and now engaged them in a ferocious duel. Finally breaking through the goblins, Avana and Finris reached the group of horsemen. They were too late. One of the goblin's blades had found its mark and Ruskin now bent over with the sword through his chest.

Avana felt tears of grief well in her eyes as she led the horsemen, with Grayson at their head, in retreat. Pulling herself together she gathered the riders around her, and they began to fight their way back to Amaroth. The dwarves were also falling back to the city. They held the road from the goblins to permit the Guard, along with Avana and the wolves, to enter the city. Then they allowed themselves to be pushed back to the gate. There they made one last stand with Halfor and Halever at their head, giving the Guard time to arrange themselves along the walls. At a final blast of the horn of Amaroth, the gates were thrown open again to grant the dwarves refuge into the city.

Arrows from the Guard kept the goblins at bay while the last dwarves entered the surrounded city. Now that the armies were safely hidden inside the walls of Amaroth, the goblins pulled back. An uneasy break in the fighting commenced. Fires sprang up around the countryside as the goblins set blaze to any dwellings in the area. The light cast a gruesome glare over the bodies strewn across the ground, as the goblins and Trolls cackled in evil fits as each structure went up in flames.

CHAPTER 18

FROM THE WALLS OF AMAROTH, the soldiers grimly watched the goblins light their fires. Some saw their own homes set aflame. Grayson, wounded by an arrow, was being treated in the infirmary while Halever consulted with the captains of the dwarf army. Avana stood with her soldiers, next to Killian and Halfor, and a bitter taste rose in her mouth as she looked over the plains before them crawling with goblins and Trolls. For the thousandth time that day, she wished her father and the elves would appear. She realized they were desperately outnumbered, with little hope. Ruskin's death left her in charge of the city and the Guard. Now she was the High Commander. Avana didn't feel like a heroic leader; instead she felt tired and dejected. As these thoughts crossed her mind, she felt Killian slip his arm around her. Avana was grateful for the comforting gesture and leaned into him. Killian gave her a gentle squeeze and smiled a forlorn smile at her. She realized he understood how she felt and this was his way of encouraging her. Mustering a small smile of her own, she kissed him on the cheek.

Together the threesome made their way along the walls, checking the watch and giving an uplifting word here and there where it was needed. Dwarf and man alike were heartened at the sight of the three brave warriors. Wherever they trod, hope sprang again into despondent hearts. After they had gone round the walls, they went into the sick bays to speak to the wounded and cheer the healers. They saw to Captain Grayson, finding that his injury had been well tended and he was resting quietly. Avana asked about supplies and how well space in the infirmaries was holding out. She was pleased to find they were short on nothing and there was still plenty of room. It was late in the evening when they retired for the night. Avana made her way to her uncle Grayson's house that butted up to the city wall. She was barely able to pull her armor off before falling down on a cot, utterly spent. She plunged into sleep instantly.

Her respite was not long however. In the wee dark hours of the morning Killian shook her awake as the horn of Amaroth sounded in warning. The goblins were attacking again, this time with grappling hooks and ladders they had fashioned in the night. Avana hastily pulled on her armor and buckled her sword around her waist. Killian had brought her a loaf of bread, and she hurriedly ate snatches of it with mouthfuls of water from her waterskin. Above her she could hear the violent cries of goblins and clash of weapons. Swiftly ascending the stairs, she found herself caught up in the melee as goblins attempted to push their way over the walls.

All around Avana and Killian, warriors worked relentlessly to throw down every ladder that was pushed up against the wall. In a terrible swarm the goblins would climb any ladder that wasn't knocked down. Once on the wall, they fought wildly, seeking to destroy the defenses of Amaroth. Running from one place to another, Avana fended off each attack with Killian at her side. She fought with blade, knife, and arrow—changing from one weapon to another as the battle called for it. On the walls on the far side of the city, Avana could see the shapes of Halever and Halfor in the harsh glare of the watch fires doing the same. As the horizon began to pale in the east into a gray dusk that then faded to a faint pink, the goblins momentarily ceased their attacks. They withdrew into a seething mass, babbling malevolent cries before the gates.

Avana wondered what devilry they were up to next. She didn't have to wait to be enlightened. Four great Trolls came through the ranks of goblins carrying a monstrous tree trunk to use as a battering ram.

"Archers! To the gate!" Avana cried out as she watched the Trolls pick up speed as they neared the gateway of Amaroth. Racing to the ramparts above the doorway, men and dwarves alike assembled, raining down a salvo of arrows on the Trolls. Bawling in protest, the great beasts continued on even as their hides grew thick with shafts. With a thunderous BOOM!, the tree hit the gate, causing the wood to shiver on impact. Drawing back for another attempt at the gate, one of the Trolls fell. An arrow had pierced its eye and traveled into the Troll's brain, killing it instantly. This threw off the other Trolls who now struggled with their heavy burden.

Avana knew the gate could not stand many more strikes like this. She faced Killian. "We will lose the wall if they get through the gate. We must push them back."

"Indeed!" Killian agreed with her. "Shall we again ride out with our wolf friends? I think though if help does not come, it will be the end for us." He finished with a somber smile.

"Let us join them one last time," Avana uttered bravely. "Yes, it shall be our end, so let it then be a great one!"

Sounding her horn in a proud blast, she summoned the wolves and their riders. Met in the street by Halfor and Halever, she explained her plan to drive the goblins from the gates. She bid the dwarf lords to stay in the city and take the remaining citizens in retreat back to the mountain if their charge failed. Halfor did not like shirking from a fight, but he also knew someone would be needed to lead the survivors to safety and continue the battle when the time came. The two dwarves embraced Avana and Killian in a gesture of farewell. Dawn was beginning in earnest to the east, and Avana knew there was no time to waste.

Once more mounting Finris, Avana drew Stelenacht, and it flamed brightly in the light of dawn. "Open the gates!" she roared. Then, with a terrific yell and carrying Stelenacht high above her head, she and Finris charged headlong out into the waiting goblin hordes. Behind her, snarling and howling, the wolves rushed out and set upon the goblins with such fury that they were pushed back many paces. Their victory was short-lived. The sheer number of goblins began to cut them off from the wall of the city.

Suddenly, from the far horizon behind the goblins, came the golden winding of a horn. Over the hills an army marched into view. The rays of morning sun shone on the ranks of soldiers marching toward them. Arrayed in light greens overlaid with bright silver armor, it was the elves who came at last! Avana's heart rocketed with renewed hope as the goblins recoiled in gibbering terror at the oncoming force.

At the head of the approaching army rode Caleb and Valanter. Valanter was tall, even by elven standards. He rode a pure white horse, and his long hair nearly matched the color of his steed. His armor was impossibly close fitted, leaving no point of weakness. It too was made of gleaming silver, but upon the breastplate, a wild stag was outlined in glittering blue gems. Accompanying the elves were sixty Rangers led by Avana's grandfather, Aramis. Clad in earthen hues upon sturdy horses, the Rangers appeared as a dark spot in front of the shining elven warriors. In contrast to Valanter's white charger, Aramis rode a burly black horse covered in dark armor. Aramis, like Valanter, was a tall man, and though advanced in years, he still sat proudly upon his horse. His hair and beard were gray, but his eyes still gleamed a vibrant blue.

Another shivering blast came from the horn of the elves, and as one they swept down upon the waiting goblins and Ice Trolls. Heartened at the sight of the oncoming army, wolves and riders alike attacked the enemy with renewed energy. Now the goblins were pressed from both the front and back. Striving mightily, the warriors drove the goblins back up against Lonrach Lake.

The elves fought with deadly grace as their lithe forces pushed forward. Soon the elves and Rangers joined the ranks of Avana's wolf fighters and they united as one force to pin their enemy along the lake. Valanter fought with a long slim sword. The ease of his movements gave the impression he was dancing instead of fighting in a deadly battle. Caleb and Aramis fought side by side as father and son. A perfect match—complimenting each other's every move.

As they battled, Killian noted how Avana nearly mirrored her kin in fighting style. They all had a relaxed manner when fighting, yet drove on relentlessly. Even small details, like how she carried her sword, were similar to her sire and grandsire. *Blood runs thick in her line*, Killian told himself, as he admired the family's prowess.

Avana and Killian had dismounted from Finris and Fallon to further pressure the goblins. Pressing onward to the very center of the battle, they found themselves facing Garzvahl himself. The goblin chieftain was tall and heavy limbed. He was dressed in black armor with a wicked- looking curved scimitar. Garzvahl was an impressive fighter and his height gave him a decisive advantage. He also was fearless, and this lent him great strength. Taking on both Killian and Avana at the same time, he held them at bay with dismaying ease. His attacks were cunning.

Garzvahl drew one opponent in, compelling the other to lend aid while leaving their back unprotected to the goblins fighting around them. Three times Garzvahl was nearly able to trap Avana and Killian. On the fourth attempt, he battered Avana mercilessly, using his stature to force her to her knees. Killian rushed in with his blade, leaving his side and arm unprotected while trying to defend Avana. Seizing the opportunity, one of Garzvahl's guards gave him a stinging blow across his shoulder, causing a dark stain to appear.

When Avana realized Killian was injured, her wrath grew to a fever pitch. Recklessly, she hammered away at Garzvahl, Stelenacht pulsing blue the entire time. With great swinging upward strokes, she beat him back and regained her footing. The heat of her attack surprised him. Caught off guard, he stumbled as she jumped to her feet. Avana drove Stelenacht deep into his thigh. He snarled at her in pain and anger. Garzvahl clutched at his leg, staggering backward into the protection of his guards. It was a crippling blow that forced his guards to pull him back from the front lines of the battle. Avana drove wildly after them, but the goblins were too many and soon swallowed up their leader in their ranks. Avana now separated from Killian, hoped desperately that he was alright. With their leader injured the goblins quickly fell back.

A horn blast from Amaroth heralded Svengale and Blane with riders mounted on fresh horses coming out of the city. This new attack, coupled with the loss of their leader, sent the goblins scurrying toward the Thraicin River that emptied into Lonrach Lake. The army from Amaroth pushed forward with gladdened hearts. They chased the goblins with such ferocity that nearly all the creatures crossed the waterway. Any left on the close side were destroyed. A troubled respite claimed both sides of the Thraicin. The armies regrouped, but neither made a move to cross over. Avana found Finris and swung up onto his back again. Svengale, Blane, and Spear soon joined her and Finris, waiting tensely for the battle to renew.

Suddenly, from the skies above, hundreds of large black crows descended on them, pecking and clawing viciously. The archers were obliged to take on this new flying foe leaving the soldiers unprotected. The goblins pursued this advantage. In a rush they streamed across the river. Soon they surrounded the army, hounding them until they were backed along the lake.

With Lonrach behind them they were cut off from escape. The flow of goblins quickly separated Avana from her men. Avana and Finris found themselves fighting alongside Valanter. The elf lord appraised Avana with cool eyes, assessing her abilities. This young maiden was fulfilling the prophecy of old. He was sure she was the one. Had she not brought the races together to fight against the goblins? Valanter did not intend to die at the hands of the murderous creatures when such a prophecy predicted victory. But as the battle unfolded, they needed help. Valanter's mind was keen and his memory long. Things forgotten by men and dwarves were not so easily left behind by elves. An ancient story stirred in the back of his mind.

There were more fabled creatures in the land than just Northern Wolves and Ice Trolls. He cast a glance at the lake behind them. He knew what lived beneath the clear waters. Valanter wondered if it would still answer in their time of need. Nonetheless, this was a desperate time, and they must have help in order to defeat the goblins.

Valanter called out to Avana in a melodious voice above the battle din, "Daughter of Caleb, hear me now. We shall not win this fight without help. I ask you now to use your heritage and birthright to save us. Call upon the dragon of Lonrach Lake!"

Avana reeled aboard Finris as she heard Valanter's words. "A dragon?" was her shocked response, and Finris growled long and low beneath her.

"Yes, a dragon, one that is linked to you. Only the king can summon the dragon. You are the heir to the lost kingdom and fulfiller of the prophecy. It is your right to do so," the elf king answered.

"But how do I summon it?" Avana asked in frustrated skepticism.

Valanter gave her a piercing look, "Take your sword and strike the water. The dragon will either answer, or he will not. If he does not, then we shall perish."

Avana swallowed her doubts in the face of the elf king's assurance. Finris turned around and they snaked their way through the madness and sought the lake's edge. When they reached the water, Avana dismounted from Finris. Holding Stelenacht in both hands, Avana stepped into the water. It lapped coldly around her legs, a refreshing shock from the furious heat of battle. Not knowing what else to do, she brought the sword over her head, and crying out the sword's name, struck the water sending a fine spray up.

Instantly, when the sword touched the water, the entire lake lit up a brilliant blue as if struck by lightning. The ground surrounding the lake quivered with an enormous shudder causing the armies of both sides to stagger. Lonrach Lake seethed and bubbled like a gigantic cauldron in front of Avana. She quickly jumped out of the lake and backtracked to Finris who was whining in apprehension.

As she watched, a massive form began to appear from the depths of the lake. The head of a cobalt colored dragon took shape as water streamed down its flashing scales. Great green eyes fixed themselves on Avana as the rest of the dragon's body began to rise above the water. Immense wings, covered in water plants, lifted and stretched like a cat waking from a nap as the dragon arched its back. With a shake of its vast body, the dragon sent algae and water flying. Abruptly, the dragon launched itself into the sky. Its wings snapped open with a rush of air that nearly flattened Avana. Up and up it went. Then, with a roar so loud it reverberated off the mountains, it spat a long eruption of flames and came hurtling down at the armies below it.

The dragon soaring above them, the armies, both good and evil, drew back in fright. "Fall back!" yelled Valanter in a voice that brooked no question. Elves, men, and wolves pulled back from the goblin lines. With a shriek, the dragon dropped down on the goblins and Trolls, crashing through them and sending their bodies flying. Its tail sliced through their ranks like a colossal sickle. The dragon reared up and a stream of flames came gurgling from its mouth, sweeping over the goblins in a wild inferno.

Avana watched in awe as the dragon again leapt into the air. It flew low over the goblin army, using its massive claws to mow down the enemy, throwing them every which way. The crows attacked the dragon only to be incinerated with a fiery blast. Goblin archers rained a hail of arrows that bounced harmlessly off the dragon's shimmering scales. The dragon was unmindful of the barrage, instead it attacked even more fiercely than before. In little time the goblin forces were decimated, and the creatures scattered before the angry dragon.

Avana and Valanter's forces chased their foul foe, intent to let none escape. The dragon too hunted the remaining goblins. It was not till the last creature was dead or in hiding that the dragon returned to the lakeside. Avana and Valanter had regrouped there. The dragon landed before them, its light agility belying its size. Emerald green eyes surveyed the army before it.

Then with a voice like a rushing river, the dragon commanded, "King's heir, come forward!"

Trembling, Avana left Finris and approached the dragon, staring up at the gigantic beast.

"What is your name, heir? I would know who summoned me," the dragon lowered its head, eyeing her curiously.

"I am Avana, Commander of the Guard and daughter of Caleb, the Ranger," Avana replied in a wavering voice.

The dragon harrumphed low in its throat. "So you're the reason my sleep has been disturbed of late! I've sensed your presence for quite some time, but I was unsure why it should bother me. I see now. You are the fulfillment of the old prophecy. I should know. It is I who gave it. I am surprised I did not realize who you were sooner. I'm sorry I did not aid you earlier." The dragon bowed its head in a submissive gesture as it apologized.

"I don't think I understand, great dragon . . ."Avana said.

Fixing on her with one bright eye, the dragon replied, "I see that you don't know your history. Many lifetimes ago I pledged to protect the kings after one of them did a great deed for me. That tale is for another time. Needless to say, I was the guardian of the ancient kingdoms and for hundreds of years I did so successfully. I saw the rise and fall of countless rulers and diligently aided them against enemies. Nonetheless, a day came when the powers of darkness became too great even for me to defend against. The kingdom of Amaroth fell, but I spirited away King Justinian, his wife Thea, and their children. The Wild Wolves of the North hid them, and they became the Rangers you see today. In return for my inability to save the kingdom I was able to instead give them hope for the future with the prophecy. Ever since then I have been asleep at the bottom of the lake waiting for the heir to fulfill the prophecy. You are that heir, Avana."

Avana was stunned by the dragon's revelation. "But what does it all mean, dragon?" she asked, still bewildered.

"It means you are the rightful ruler of men, and all of Arda's people owe you their allegiance," the dragon answered with authority.

"I have no wish to rule though," Avana countered with uncertainty. "I know nothing of leading a kingdom."

The dragon gave a rumbling laugh. "You just led an entire army in battle. You know more than you think, young one. But humility is a prized quality in a ruler. You will do well."

Avana struggled to wrap her mind around the dragon's words. She was the Queen of Arda? It seemed so odd, yet so many other strange things had happened to her that it didn't seem so impossible now. She realized, though, she had forgotten to ask the dragon an important question, "Please, dragon, do you have a name?" she asked respectfully.

"My name is Zellnar, dragon of Lonrach Lake, and yours to command," he replied with a slight bow.

Feeling a bit braver, Avana drew close to Zellnar and reached out, placing her hand on his leg as he towered above her. His scales were smooth and supple, reminding Avana of a snakeskin, yet they were infinitely hard with no spaces between them. He radiated a heat that flowed into Avana and warmed her from head to toe. She could also feel the magic coming from him, causing her to realize all the more that he was no ordinary being.

"Thank you for saving us, Zellnar," Avana said gratefully after a moment. "We would not have survived without your help."

Looking down at her, Zellnar gave a sharp-toothed smile. "You're welcome, Avana. It was good to be wakened after so many years of deep slumber."

Avana was quiet for a few moments before speaking. "So what will you do now? Will you go back to sleep?"

"No! Not for a while, at least. I am hungry so I must hunt. Besides, I'd like to make sure all of the goblin scum have been accounted for," Zellnar answered eagerly. "But if you ever need me, just touch the lake with your sword, and I will know you are calling me."

Avana gave the dragon a winning smile, "Again, thank you, Zellnar. I must return now, but I am pleased to have met you. What I have learned from you I will not take lightly. Farewell!" With a bow to Zellnar, she then returned to the waiting company.

She looked back when she felt a great rush of wind as the dragon again took to the skies. Avana watched as he wheeled and with a fierce cry, went streaking toward the Wilds skyline.

CHAPTER 19

WITH VALANTER AND HER MEN, they began to take account of all who were left and all who were wounded. Avana was overjoyed to find Killian in stable condition, though his wound had been deep. Many good men, dwarves, wolves, and elves had been lost over the last few days. Though they rejoiced at their victory over the goblins, they were filled with sorrow for their fallen friends. Avana cried unashamedly when she learned both Tam and Griff were killed that day. Of her other six friends, only Svengale had not been badly wounded, and Mattson was the worst with a head injury that left him unconscious. She also grieved over the loss of Commander Ruskin. She would miss his stern voice and wise words. Most of all, Avana would miss him as her friend. They spent the day honoring the fallen and lighting funeral pyres so that birds and beasts would not get to the bodies.

They also made a survey of the countryside around Amaroth. Most of it was completely ransacked by the goblins. It would take a great deal of rebuilding and replanting to bring everything back. A message was sent out to the people who fled to the Tiered Mountain that it was safe to return. Those left in Amaroth began the tedious process of tearing down the barricades and defenses set up throughout the city. Valanter and Halfor both pitched in to help rebuild the houses and farms around Amaroth.

Slowly the people came back from the mountains, and rebuilding began in earnest. The time now came for Amaroth's allies to begin to leave. The packs were the first to depart. Though Avana pleaded with Finris that they stay longer, he would not hear of it.

"The city is no place for a Wild Wolf," Finris told her gently. He promised the pack would never be far from her, and she was welcome to visit whenever she wished.

A week after the battle, Valanter left with his army of elves and returned to the Greenwood. Avana's grandfather Aramis and the Rangers set forth soon after. They wished to spread out and search for any goblins that possibly escaped back to their holes. It was a somber parting between father, son, and granddaughter. Avana did not know Aramis well, but she felt a strong connection to him since she had lost the rest of her family. Aramis praised Avana and her courage in battle. He encouraged her to accept her heritage, and if the leadership of all Amaroth was offered to her, to take it.

"I believe it is time to take back the throne, Avana." Aramis spoke firmly. "I know that you do not wish to rule, nor do you feel ready, but the peoples of Arda will be looking for your leadership. Don't be afraid!"

Avana was unsure how to respond to her grandfather's words, but she thanked him for his confidence in her. Avana and Caleb bid Aramis farewell and watched as he and the Rangers rode from the city back into the Wilds.

Troubled by Aramis's words, Avana turned to Caleb and said, "Wouldn't the right to rule make more sense falling to you, Father? You are older and wiser. You have much more experience. After all, you too held a great sword and a wolf skin."

"Nay, daughter," Caleb answered with solemn eyes. "My chance has long gone. I did not wish to take it. Now it falls to you. You will do much better than I."

Avana shook her head, feeling overwhelmed by his words. She wasn't sure if, when the time came for her to rule, she would be ready. As she contemplated Aramis and Caleb's words, she remembered something.

"Father, did Valanter give you a new sword?" Avana asked anxiously.

Caleb smiled broadly and unfastened the scabbard at his waist. Holding it out, he withdrew a beautiful sword. It was dark in color, a smoky charcoal instead of shining silver. It had writings in black letters scripted upon it. White gemstones in the pommel were the only source of brightness to be seen.

"Behold! This is Ristfaeth, or Reckoning. I named it so because of the battle that was to be fought and in remembrance of the past. It served me well. Nedanael made it for me and told me of his rescue and meeting with you. This sword is part of the reason for our late arrival. Valanter would not march until the sword was forged for me, though I pressed him to leave immediately. I think he must have wanted you to call upon the dragon at the end. The sword only gave him an excuse to delay. Elves know many things because they are immortal beings. I believe that he had seen this day coming," Caleb said.

"But why would he wish me to call Zellnar?" Avana considered curiously.

"Because it would prove that you are the true heir to the throne. Valanter wanted the whole world to see once and for all that you are the rightful queen. By summoning the dragon, no one can dispute your authority," Caleb spoke plainly.

Again, Avana felt unsure of this confidence, but she pushed her thoughts and feelings aside. She had much to do as the Commander of the Guard and couldn't afford to let her emotions cloud her judgment. Avana and Caleb returned to the city and continued to help repair damages and restore homes.

Halfor and the dwarves stayed on for another week after the elves left. They skillfully mended the broken bits of wall and any stone structures destroyed by the goblins. Eventually, they too headed back for their own homes. Killian went with them because he was needed back in the dwarf kingdom—there were many matters to settle after the defeat of the goblins. Avana did not want him to leave, but she knew his first priority was to his king and his people.

This parting was the hardest of all for Avana. Her love for Killian had only grown during the past time of adventures and battle. When the hour came for them to part, she shed no tears. Though her heart was forlorn, she felt that no tears should be cried for the living after the losses they had so recently suffered. Instead, she looked on bravely as Killian marched off toward the Cascade Mountains with Halfor and Halever. They had promised each other to continue with their correspondence until they met again.

With the aid of Caleb and her uncle Grayson, Avana focused on her duties as Commander of the Guard in earnest. The Guard needed a strong leader as they recovered from the terrible battle. Looters needed to be dealt with as they tried to take advantage of the partially emptied city. It wouldn't do to have families return to homes that were pillaged.

She delegated the task of clean up to Captain Grayson, who was making a rapid recovery, while the robbers and looters she gave over to Svengale, Blane and her remaining men. Mattson had eventually come out of his coma, but he was still required to stay in the infirmary. Therefore, Avana gave him the job of taking an inventory of the supplies left after the battle. Avana herself had to deal with the Elders of the city. These men were pompous, yet powerful. Most fled when the news of the goblins reached Amaroth, but a few of the bravest remained. These men had holed up in secure locations and surrounded themselves with many guards. Now that Ruskin was gone, Avana was considered one of them, but it was taking a great deal of convincing to secure their respect.

Though they were grateful to have their city back safely, they were loath to listen to the advice of some young woman. The Elders were power hungry, and it galled them that Avana had joined their ranks so easily. The people of Amaroth felt differently. They were extremely grateful to Avana and she was revered among them. They loved her, and no matter what the rest of the Elders said, popular opinion always swayed toward Avana.

Months passed as Amaroth continued to rebuild and start anew in the aftermath of the battle. Avana found the Guard to be severely depleted of men, as hundreds had been lost in the war. So she began a determined recruiting campaign to replace as many soldiers as possible. Avana was surprised when countless young people from the area answered her call. She had not thought such a number would want to join, but her fame gave her an immense advantage. Few wished to be left out of the army commanded by the famous warrior.

As the year drew to a close, Grayson asked if he could speak to Avana privately. Ushering him into her office, she sat down expectantly.

Captain Grayson looked uncomfortable as he stood across from her. He shuffled his feet trying to decide how to best explain his subject. Finally, he blurted out, "I wish to retire."

Avana studied him in surprise for a long minute, and then asked, "Why do you wish to retire, Uncle? You are a valuable soldier! I rely on you greatly."

"Because I am getting old, Avana. This last battle was enough for me to see that. I love the way of the warrior, but time is catching up with me. My dwarf blood may still give me many years of life, however I would prefer to not live them on battle campaigns. The cold and wet along with sleeping on the hard ground are getting to be a bit much for these old bones. I have served the Guard for most of my life. I would fight again if you called upon me in a time of need, but I am ready to lead a more relaxed life," Grayson said with great fatigue.

Avana replied kindly, "I understand, Uncle Grayson. I meant no offense. I simply wanted to make sure that you are settled in this matter. You deserve retirement. You will be missed, though."

Grayson gave her a relieved smile and answered, "Thank you for understanding. I would be happy to advise you in any matter in which you need counsel."

Avana rose and walked to her uncle. She hugged him and spoke proudly, "The Guard will have a celebration to commemorate you. Your retirement will not go unnoticed!"

Grayson tried to brush aside her idea, but Avana would not allow it. Instead she called in Blane to begin arrangements for the retirement party. The entire Guard turned out to celebrate Grayson. Speeches were given and toasts were made to Grayson and his deeds of service. To end the evening, Avana bestowed upon Grayson the title of Captain Emeritus as a sign of distinction. She also named Caleb as his successor. This was agreeable to all in the Guard. It had taken a great deal of convincing from Avana and Grayson to persuade Caleb to take the position, but in the end he agreed. As the night drew to a close, Avana felt satisfied with the events that transpired. The job of leading the Guard was beginning to run smoothly; now her greatest challenge was tussling with the other Elders.

While Avana was busy in Amaroth, Killian too found himself heavily occupied. It was never easy to set things back to right when lives were lost. Halfor made Killian one of his advisors and the highest-ranking general in his army. This in itself made a hectic schedule, but there was something else that caused Killian distraction. He was building a house. Though he employed other dwarves to help him, he often worked on it alone. Killian wanted the home to be faultless and paid great attention to detail, creating a charming abode.

Finally the house was finished. Now Killian could turn his attentions to the most important detail of all, forging a ring for Avana. He spent days pouring over countless designs, creating dozens of prototypes in wax, and refining the ring's form. At last he hit on the perfect one. Again, more hours were spent as he carefully crafted the band. When completed, he placed it in a small delicately inlaid box that he carried in his pocket.

During this time Avana and Killian kept up their letters. Killian did not mention to her his personal work. As the next year commenced, Avana's letters became more sparse and her words more formal. One thing remained consistent in them, however. In every letter she spoke of her trouble with the Elders.

In her latest letter to Killian, Avana made mention of the possibility of her becoming Queen. It had been almost two years since the battle against the goblins, and the people wanted to see a ruler restored to the throne. The Elders of course did not approve of this. It had been suggested to Avana that perhaps she should marry one of them before ascending to the throne. Nothing was to be decided, however, until a Council was called. Avana's letter invited Killian to the Council meeting, stating he had the right to be there.

The tone of Avana's latest letter was distant and unemotional. Killian was now exceedingly worried. Was all his hard work and love to come to nothing? Had Avana succumbed to the pride and pressures of power? Killian decided the only way to answer his question was to attend the Council as Avana requested.

Killian quickly prepared for his trip so he could join the

Council at the appointed time. Making his way to Amaroth, Killian was troubled. What lay ahead of him? Would Avana reject him after all? These thoughts and more filled his mind as he journeyed onward.

CHAPTER 20

WHEN HE REACHED THE CITY THAT NIGHT, he made for the Highwater Inn and dispatched a message to Avana, letting her know he arrived in Amaroth. He soon received a note from her asking him to meet on the east wall of the city. Killian thought this a strange place to meet, but hastily sent a reply of agreement. Presently, Killian found himself on the high wall surrounding Amaroth. Only the sentries were about, but none questioned him on his business. Peering into the darkness, he saw a shrouded figure approaching him.

It was Avana, clad in dark garments, with her cloak pulled tightly around her. Upon seeing Killian, she flew to him, throwing her arms around him and kissed him passionately. At this welcome, all of Killian's fears disappeared, and he held Avana close.

Pulling back, Avana finally spoke contritely, "I'm sorry for my strange letters and this unpleasant meeting place. The Elders have been after me. I believe they've been intercepting my mail. I did not wish to give them anything they could use against me. Please forgive me. The Elders have committed many treacherous acts to keep me from becoming Queen. My father and I haven't been able to prove anything until now. That's why we agreed to this Council meeting. We intend to unmask them. It would be most fitting for you to be there."

Killian was surprised by her answer. He hadn't realized the

situation had become so grim. He was glad he had come when Avana asked. "What do you need me to do?"

"Mostly, I need you to support my claim to the throne. Also, I could use a friend," Avana said blushing. "One of the Elders has proposed to me three times! I have turned him down, but he has become more and more insistent. I'm afraid it will escalate. I can't marry him. I love you, Killian, and no one else."

Killian smiled at Avana as a plan formed in his mind. "I would be glad to support you. You can count on me being at the Council. I will back up your claim."

Avana beamed at him. "Thank you, Killian. I knew I could count on you. I must leave now. I doubt we'll be able to see each other again before the Council. I can't afford to let them see us together. I'm sorry it has to be this way," she repeated in frustration.

"Don't be sorry. Soon you will take your rightful place, and it won't matter what the Elders think." Killian assured her, taking her hand and giving it a squeeze. After another quick embrace, he watched Avana hurry back the way she came. Killian had a lot to think about after their meeting. He was angry the Elders were disputing her claim to the throne. He also knew that, if it came down to it, Avana could call on Finris and Zellnar to validate her title, but that she did not wish to do so unless it was the greatest need. She'd want to prove her claim on her own merit. Killian walked on the wall for some time, pondering more on what Avana said. The Council was to be held the day after tomorrow, and he hoped nothing would happen before then.

The following day passed quickly, and the time was now at hand for Killian to attend the Council. Killian spent a great deal of the previous day speaking with Grayson to learn all that he could about the Elders. He was not surprised by what Grayson told him. All of the Elders were power hungry men who did not wish to give up their positions. Clearly they were going to make things as difficult for Avana as possible.

The Council meeting was to take place in a great banquet hall in the center of the city. It was a magnificent building, designed to host feasts for visiting dignitaries. The meeting itself was to be held in a smaller upper room. Though it was not the largest of meeting places, it was no less beautiful, with colonnades and balconies filled with hanging flowers. Killian had dressed in his finest clothes and was met by footmen at the door of the building. He was escorted upstairs where a long table was laid out lavishly with a sumptuous meal. Killian knew all of this luxury was a show, designed to make it clear to Avana that Amaroth did not need her as Queen.

Killian was seated toward the far end of the table near Caleb and several other men he vaguely recognized. It was obvious who the Elders were. The six Elders sat at the opposite end of the table from Killian, and kept to themselves. They were clothed in the best linens and silks. Each man had an abundance of jewels worn on their fingers, clothes, and around their necks. They varied greatly in age, but none could have been younger than forty. Avana had not arrived yet, and Killian could tell the Elders were dissatisfied with her late appearance.

Serves them right, Killian thought. *She should make them wait as long as she likes.*

A short rap on the door gained everyone's attention. The footman entered the room announcing the arrival of Avana. Caleb and the other men stood at his announcement, and Killian did the same. He noticed the Elders remained seated as Avana walked into the room. Avana looked absolutely regal. She was clad in a deep green dress that hugged her body and fell in a shimmering trail behind her. A cloak of the same color, but streaked with silver, complemented her dress. She wore knee high, fitted, black leather boots that allowed her to walk soundlessly over the floor. Her chestnut hair had been carefully curled and cascaded in waves down her back. Stelenacht was buckled at her waist as a sign of her position as Commander of the Guard. Around her neck, to Killian's delight, she wore the necklace he bought her years ago.

Avana regarded the room with a cool glance. She stared coolly at the men before her. With a level voice she spoke, "You may be seated," and nodded carefully to the standing men. As one they quickly sat back down at the table. Giving the Elders at the head of the table an icy glare, Avana made her way to the empty seat waiting for her. Now that she arrived, the meal began. Though the food was excellent, the conversation was formal and shallow. Killian could see that Caleb was becoming agitated with the inactivity and he hoped Avana's father would not speak before the time was right.

Finally the meal was at an end, and the Elders seemed to gather themselves to begin their attack. The youngest of them, a tall dark haired man clad in deep blues with handsome features, stood up from the table. Raising a hand he quieted the conversations.

With a haughty look around the table, he began, "Thank you all for coming to this Council. I believe we all know the reason for this meeting, but I feel it is necessary for posterity for us to restate the issue. We have gathered today regarding the claim of Avana, Commander of the Guard, and daughter of the Ranger, Caleb, to the throne. We, the Elders of this city, do not want to take such a claim lightly and therefore have looked into this matter with the utmost care." He was interrupted by a rude snort from one of the men at Killian's end of the table.

Glaring at the man in annoyance, the Elder continued, "I, Ellias, and the rest of our esteemed Elders, have concluded that Avana does have the rightful claim to the throne."

A collective gasp went up from those around the far end of the table. Caleb whispered rapidly to the man seated next to him as they debated this new turn of events. Only Avana seemed unperturbed. She simply nodded her head in a small measure of assent.

Ellias cleared his throat and continued, "However, we have done some research into the ascension of a monarch in situations such as this." A crafty smile spread across his countenance.

Killian and the rest of the men listened with renewed interest and tension.

"According to the ancient law of the land, a monarch ascending to a throne that was not directly passed on to them by a previous ruling king or queen must be married to a member of the Court. Since there is no longer a Court of the king, we believe it is only right that Avana wed someone of this Council, with myself as the obvious choice," Ellias finished, looking smug.

Pandemonium broke out around Killian as the Elders looked on arrogantly with self-satisfied airs. Caleb stalked angrily up to Ellias and began arguing with him, gesticulating wildly. The other men also fell upon the rest of the Elders, questioning them closely with hot words. Killian was shocked by the news from the Elders, but unlike the others, he chose to sit and quietly digest the information. He perceived that Avana paled at Ellias's announcement, but kept her composure. She too sat quietly, watching the mayhem around her.

After a few moments she spoke in a commanding voice, "Peace, everyone! Elders, I ask that you give me some time to consider your words. I will retire to the balcony and shall give you an answer when I return."

"Agreed! We will give you all the time you need," Ellias answered condescendingly.

Avana rose from her chair and walked to the farthest balcony, disappearing through the curtains into the darkness beyond. Slowly, the voices of the men began to rise in anger again as the arguments continued after Avana's departure. Killian waited for ten minutes or so, allowing everyone to become deeply involved in their discussions, before walking purposefully after Avana. In the heat of the moment, no one noticed the dwarf as he slipped out onto the balcony.

Passing through the curtains, he beheld Avana sitting pensively on the edge of the rail looking out over Amaroth.

In a detached, impassive voice, Avana spoke. "I know your footsteps, dwarf. You cannot hide your presence from me. I also know you wish to give me counsel, but this burden is mine alone." She gracefully alighted from the rail and stood facing Killian with a blank expression.

Killian was taken aback by her emotionless manner, but he pressed on. "Indeed, Avana, I wish to aid you." He said with a courtly bow.

"And how can you aid me?" Avana asked in a distant voice, looking down on Killian.

Swallowing his fear, Killian dropped to one knee and reached into his pocket. He pulled out a box that contained an exquisite ring. With all the courage he could muster he held it out to Avana and asked, "Avana, Commander of the Guard, daughter of Caleb, will you marry me?"

Avana's eyes widened in astonishment as a flood of emotions rushed through them. Of course! This was the answer to Ellias and the Elders. After all, they had said she must marry someone from the Council. She couldn't imagine spending her life with anyone other than Killian.

"Yes! Yes, I will marry you!" Avana said as tears gathered in her eyes and warmth spread through her. Killian watched as the wave of emotions washed over Avana. Gone was the cold woman of a few moments ago. His heart danced with joy over Avana's answer. With great care he placed the ring on her finger. It sparkled brilliantly in the evening starlight. Forgetting decorum, Killian let his elation run away with him and he pulled Avana into an ardent kiss. For a minute the world fell away, but the spell was soon broken by the raised voices behind them.

Drawing back from Killian, Avana squared her shoulders and faced the curtains separating them from the hall. Wordlessly, she stalked back into the room with Killian close behind her. The chamber quieted with her arrival and all eyes were upon her.

In a clear voice, Avana said, "I have made my decision. I am pleased to announce my engagement to Killian, son of Kalmar, and nephew of the Dwarf King Halfor."

Cheers and applause rose from the men who supported Avana, but the Elders looked outraged. Ellias spluttered in anger, "But you must be engaged to someone on this Council, Avana!" meaning the Elders sitting around him.

"Precisely, Ellias," Avana answered, allowing herself a small smile. "You said anyone on this Council. Killian is on this Council, and I have chosen him. You would not go back on your word or against the ancient law, Elder Ellias?"

Ellias was absolutely livid, but he knew he was trapped. There were too many witnesses to wriggle out of his predicament. "I would never do such a thing," he said through clenched teeth. "I believe our meeting is now adjourned, as our business has been settled. I do hope you set a wedding date soon, so we may get on with the coronation," he said in a sickly sweet voice.

"I agree. The meeting is over, "Avana stated airily.

With this statement, Ellias and the rest of the Elders stormed out of the banquet hall, leaving Avana and her followers to a happy celebration.

The next day, with great fanfare, the news spread that Avana was engaged and meant to take back the throne. The entire countryside was overjoyed with this announcement. Halfor and Valanter both sent messages filled with their happiness and congratulations for the couple. It was decided the coronation and wedding should be held on the same day. Avana was a practical person; she thought it made better sense to invite guests to a single event rather than force them to travel twice.

The date was set for eight months hence. Avana hoped this was enough time to set everything in order, but she knew she had many friends who were willing to help. One night, Avana secretly went out from the city to speak to Zellnar. She told him of all the events that had transpired and about the wedding and coronation. Avana invited the dragon, saying that he had more right than anyone to attend. Zellnar agreed, but asked that they hold the wedding outside of Amaroth. She readily concurred as she also wished to invite Finris and the other wolves.

CHAPTER 21

AVANA DECIDED SHE WANTED TO DELIVER THE NEWS to Finris and the pack personally. Avana, Killian, and Caleb traveled to the Wilds until they were a three days' ride from the city. Taking up her horn, Avana blew a long clear blast. A winding howl answered her. Avana recognized the notes in it, and knew it was Fallon.

Soon Fallon, Finris and some of the others from the wolf pack appeared. With joyous barks and growls they were happily reunited with their friends. Finris was delighted by the news. Growling affectionately, he nuzzled each of them in turn. "This is most excellent news, dearest Avana! Of course we will attend the wedding and coronation. It will be a great honor for the Wolves of the North," he finished with a bow of his head.

With a bright smile, Avana looked up at Finris and said, "I have something else important to ask you Finris. Would you carry the crown for the coronation?"

Finris grinned with his tongue out and teeth fully bared. "I can think of nothing I would like to do more for you. The honor will go down in the history of the Wild Wolves for ages to come. After this, and everything else that has happened, I do not think Arda will forget the Wild Wolves of the North. Our time as a legend is coming to an end. Perhaps we are again entering into an era of fellowship with men."

"I hope so, old friend." Caleb spoke in a confident voice. "It's time for changes, and a renewed friendship would be beneficial to all."

Avana echoed her father's sentiments, "I intend to make both you and Zellnar welcome at all times to the city. Father is right. We need to show people wolves are allies, not to be feared."

"The dwarves already wish to extend terms of friendship with your wolves, Finris," Killian said happily.

"And we would gratefully accept them," Finris replied with a pleased growl. "It is also beneficial to us to have allies to fall back on in troubled times."

They spent the rest of the day chatting and enjoying one another's company. They spent the night with the wolves before beginning their ride back to the city. Fallon accompanied them for part of the journey back to Amaroth. He missed his adopted sister, and wished to spend as much time with her as possible. Avana invited him to come and visit Amaroth anytime he wanted, but he declined. Until she became Queen, he did not think it wise for a wolf to approach the city, even in friendship.

Once they returned to Amaroth, it felt like the days leading up to the great day of celebration flew by at an impossible speed. Everything was moving so fast that Avana often had to stop and wonder if it was real. So much had happened. She had gone from a normal young girl, to a trained warrior, and finally she was to become Queen, all in the short span of time that was her life. But she also realized she was happy with how everything turned out. Avana was grateful her courage and persistence had paid off.

Finally on the big day, Avana awoke to a flutter of nerves. Her mind buzzed excitedly as she tried to eat breakfast. The wedding and coronation were to be held in the early afternoon, outside the gates of the city along the lakeside. This way, the wolves and Zellnar would be comfortable. The morning was spent in a flurry of preparations. Avana's old roommate Nora, and Killian's mother Zyphereth, helped Avana get ready. They skillfully arranged her hair and helped her, when the time came, to slip into the glittering white wedding gown.

The dress was adorned with thousands of tiny white gems and fitted her perfectly. A silver belt around her waist offset the glowing diamonds. A long train trailed behind her as she walked. Seated upon Finris and escorted by her father, Avana made her way to the gates of the city.

Trumpets sounded to announce her arrival as they came through the gates. A beautiful flowered archway rose above a wide, covered platform. Many chairs had been set up for all of the guests. It seemed the entire city had turned out along with many dwarves and elves. Halfor and Valanter both sat in places of honor at the front. Hundreds of wolves gathered, and off to the side, Zellnar lay watching the proceedings with his great green eyes.

A long aisle had been created leading to the platform. When they reached the aisle, Avana dismounted from Finris and hugged him. Taking Caleb's arm, she turned her attention to what lay before her. Aramis was to officiate the wedding and beamed at her from his place on the platform. Standing next him was Killian, wearing the finest black leathers accented with gold, his eyes shining as he watched Avana walk toward him. Avana's heart swelled with joy as she made her way to him.

Caleb gave his daughter's hand to the dwarf, and his eyes were bright with unshed tears of pride and love. The ceremony was short and to the point. The couple spoke their vows of love and faithfulness binding them together. They shared a quick kiss to seal their marriage before moving on to the next part of the ceremony. Killian stepped down from the platform, beaming at his new bride. With a strong tug he pulled on a large rope. The ceiling of the platform fell gracefully back, leaving them in the open air.

Aramis too stepped down, leaving Avana alone on the platform, where Zellnar had come up to the edge. His deep blue scales twinkled like sapphires in the sun. With his resonant rumbling voice, he said, "Avana, daughter of Caleb, and rightful heir to the throne, do you accept the responsibility of leadership and protection to all the people of Amaroth and any others who swear allegiance to you?"

"I do," Avana answered simply.

"Do you promise to judge fairly to the best of your abilities and uphold the law?" Zellnar asked.

"I do," Avana repeated.

"Then as is my right, I do declare you the Queen of Amaroth and the surrounding Wilds. Finris, please bring forward the crown," Zellnar commanded in a rolling voice.

Finris brought the crown up to Avana. Aramis took it from him and stepped back onto the platform to stand in front of Avana. She knelt before him, and he placed the crown on her head.

With a voice like a thundering waterfall, Zellnar declared, "All hail, Queen Avana!"

The crowds echoed his words with a loud shout and applause. The wolves sent up a great chorus of howls, and the noise reverberated off the city walls and the mountains. When the cheering had died down, Killian again ascended the platform and took Avana's hand. Together they walked down the aisle to the waiting tables laden with food.

A great feast was held in celebration of the wedding and coronation. Such a gathering had not been seen since the days of the kings of old. Every sort of food was available and tales of bravery were retold in honor of the two heroes who were now wed. Even Zellnar and the wolves were provided for, with dozens of whole cattle having been brought for them. It was a time of great happiness, much needed after all of the terrible things that had happened.

It was decided that Avana and Killian would split their time between Amaroth and the Tiered Mountain. It was Avana's deepest wish to spend as much time as possible in the home Killian built for them, but there was still the matter of who would be in charge during her absences. The two had put a great deal of thought into the problem and came up with the same solution.

They decided beforehand they should announce their decision during the celebration meal. Rising from the dais where she and Killian dined, Avana addressed the crowds surrounding them. "My dear friends and allies, it has been known for some time that I will spend part of my time here and part of my time in the dwarf kingdom. There has been much speculation as to who should rule in my stead while I am away. Killian and I have put great effort into making a decision. I believe, though, that it is one you will support. So, as my first official act as Queen, I do name my father, Caleb, as Regent of Amaroth and all the Wilds."

Caleb sat in stunned surprise at Avana's decree while the crowd shouted their approval. Halfor, Valanter, and the citizens of Amaroth were satisfied by Avana's choice. A good and wise man to back up the Queen would only make her more powerful and well loved.

Zellnar himself was pleased with Avana's choice and, in his rushing river voice, spoke with finality, "Well done, Your Majesty. Already you truly prove yourself to be Queen of Amaroth and all the Wilds."

It was a glorious day. Nothing could have prepared Avana for all of the challenges she had faced in her life, but with Killian at her side, she now felt ready for whatever adventures would come their way. Several days later, Avana and Killian stepped over the threshold of the lovely house Killian built for his beloved bride. Looking around her, Avana let out a happy sigh of contentment. Finally, she was home!

Acknowledgments

I wish to thank . . .

My ever so patient husband, Luke, for all the time I have sat typing away, and for him being an excellent listener as I ramble on about my story ideas. My mother, for being my first editor. My Aunt Rachel Lathrop and Aunt Peggy Woodard, for reading my book, giving helpful feedback, and encouraging me to publish my story. I also want to thank my friends, Ryan and Laura Pasveer, for loving my storyline enough to argue over my characters, asking me to clarify relationships and plotlines, and for daring me to draw my own map! To all the rest of my friends who read this book in raw form, your feedback and excitement were so appreciated. Thank you to my cousin, Caleb, for letting me steal your personality—I only hope you don't mind me making you old in the story! Thank you to my wonderful editor, Alice Osborn, for your patience and time. I would have been lost on this adventure without you.

ABOUT THE AUTHOR

Caitlin Hodnefield started writing short stories as part of her homeschool curriculum and then moved on to fantasy fanfiction in college. Caitlin lives in rural Iowa, owns Lacey, her beloved horse, and loves exploring everything that has to do with the outdoors: hiking, fishing, and archery. Archery is one of her favorite pastimes, as it requires lots of practice and sneakiness. She has been a jack-of-all-trades with jobs from taxidermy to parking lot striping. When she's not outside, you can catch her reading fantasy (of course!) with a bowl of homegrown popcorn at her side. She wishes she could meet a real dragon someday.

Made in the USA
Coppell, TX
03 March 2020